Derailed

On Track But Off Course
Book 2

Enjoy The Twins & Turns, '24 TKR

T.K. Richards

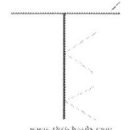

Copyright © 2022 by T.K. Richards

All rights reserved.

No part of this book may be reproduced in any form or by any electronic or mechanical means, including information storage and retrieval systems, without written permission from the author, except for the use of brief quotations in a book review.

This novel is a work of fiction with character names, places, and incidents created by the author's imagination. Any resemblance is coincidental to any event, location, or person either living or dead.

ISBN: 978-1-959253-00-6

First printing, 2022 T.K. Richards Books"

Pivot.

Chapter 1

Flag on the Play
Millicent

"I know those eyes," Millicent muttered before she screamed, alarming the neighbor's dogs. The masked face stood at her bedroom window, eerily piercing into her soul and grinning at her fright before he took off into the night.

Millicent stood frozen atop the shattered glass sporadically spread on the floor, paralyzed as her life flashed before her—The mistakes, the secrets, the betrayals, and most of all the failure of finding love. She was a catch after all: beautiful, educated, and well-off, but single and alone inside a townhouse of *picture-less* walls.

"Ms. St. James! Ms. St. James!" Her neighbor pounded at her door. "Are you alright in there? Please say something! I've called the police!"

Hopping around the broken glass, she made her way to the door and peeped through the keyhole. Back and forth her neighbor paced with the telephone pressed to her ear. Millicent flung the door open.

"Did you see anyone?! Did anyone run past you? Did you see a car at least?" she asked.

"She's opened the door. I'll wait here with her until the police arrive," her neighbor answered with the phone now pressed to her chest. "Thank God you're okay. I told the lady who answered my 911 call everything I know. I heard you scream, and my dogs went crazy. I didn't see anyone."

"Argh!" Millicent tugged at her hair.

"Why did you scream like that? If you don't mind my asking?"

"A man wearing a mask was staring at me in my window, and he threw something at me." Millicent's voice cracked.

"My Lawd. Which way did he go?"

"He took off that way," Millicent pointed towards the entrance.

Faint blue lights flashed in the distance, growing brighter once the police cars turned the corner on Millicent's street. Her neighbor placed her hand around Millicent's.

"You are more than welcome to spend the night at my house. My husband can fix your window in the morning. A woman staying alone, I am sure he will be happy to help."

"I don't feel comfortable staying anywhere close to here tonight." Tears formed in the corners of her eyes.

"But where will you go this time of night? It's times like this when being neighborly is required of the Lord."

As Millicent's neighbor repeatedly called on the Lord and squeezed her hand, Millicent wished she'd stop talking. She suffered listening to her prayers with passive commentary of her being a single woman living alone until two officers approached them. "Not such a great night it appears. Which one of you live here?"

Millicent raised her hand. "I do. Millicent St. James."

"I'm Detective Scott. This is my partner, Officer Reed. Sorry you had to call us out here tonight."

"I called," the neighbor interrupted.

"You want to tell us what made you call 911?"

While the neighbor gave her account of events, Officer Reed escorted Millicent inside. He picked up the object centered between the broken glass.

"Does this look familiar to you, Miss...?"

"St. James, and no, officer."

"Notice anyone lurking around?"

"I can't say that I have."

"Any enemies out to harm you? Kids you may have stopped playing in the street?"

"No enemies. Pretty good with kids."

"And you saw the perp. Yes?"

"I didn't see much. A man dressed in black with a ski mask over his face staring at me. When I saw him, he threw whatever that is through the window." She pointed to the mess on the floor. "I screamed, and he ran away in that direction."

"Can you estimate the height and weight of the perp?"

Millicent sighed. She had a clear idea who was terrorizing her. She stalled, contemplating if she didn't make a huge deal of the broken window, she could avoid facing her dreaded ex in court, and move on with her life. "I'd say pretty tall. Maybe five-foot-eleven, six feet tall, slender build."

Detective Scott entered Millicent's bedroom. He briefed Officer Reed on his conversation with the neighbor then suggested to Millicent, "Your neighbor mentioned she offered for you to stay with her tonight. I would advise you to take her up on her offer until you get this window fixed. Hopefully, whoever did this will slip up, and we'll have him in custody soon. Make the streets a little safer. And this is a nice neighborhood. We don't get many calls in this area."

Millicent shook her head. "I have friends in Detroit. I'm sure they wouldn't mind me staying a few nights. Can one of you stay in here with me while I pack a bag, please?"

"Certainly," said Detective Scott. "I'll be outside checking the perimeter. By chance do you have a trash bag and some tape for this window?"

"Top shelf in the pantry."

While packing, Millicent became overwhelmed and dropped a few tears. The hatred in the intruder's eyes spooked her. Her gut told her it was Miles, and her mind raced back to their breakup months ago. She thought she had seen the last of him, and buried the image of him and the embarrassment she felt from being duped by a psycho. But now his eyes found a way to haunt her forever.

Officer Reed carried her bags to the front of her house while she turned off the lights. A man-shaped silhouette appeared behind the blinds in the living room. "Ahhh!" Millicent screamed.

"My apologies! Ms. St. James, it's me, Detective Scott. I was checking your windows," he shouted through the glass before making his way inside. "Forgive me for scaring you. I was making sure your windows were locked so you'd be safe whenever you return."

Millicent placed her hands on her chest. "This is too much."

"Again, I apologize, but I also have some bad news. A witness that lives in your division said they saw someone running from your house and into the woods. I've called for backup to comb the area and see if we can find anything. And your neighbors have pointed out that your vehicle has four flat tires."

Her arms dropped to her side. Her shoulders slouched and she fell to the floor. "How the fuck am I supposed to get to Detroit now!"

The officers looked at each other.

Derailed

"I apologize. I didn't mean to curse, but fuck! What the hell is happening?!"

"I already have an officer checking your car for fingerprints. Here's hoping we find something to help catch this menace."

"Sir, excuse me for saying, but is it safe to say this wasn't random?"

Detective Scott sighed. "I agree with Reed here. It appears you were personally targeted. Any enemies that may want to..."

"We've already been there, done that." Officer Reed shook his head.

"Can one of you stay while I make some calls? It's late, but hopefully one of my friends will drive out tonight and pick me up because I can't stay here. I just can't."

Examining Millicent with a close eye, Officer Reed offered to take her to Detroit if his supervisor granted him the clearance.

"How long will that take?" Millicent asked.

"Someone's gunning for a promotion with community service." Detective Scott nudged his head to the door. "The captain's outside."

Officer Reed stepped out to speak to the captain with Millicent's bags in tow.

"Nice place you have here." Detective Scott aimed for small talk.

"Thank you. It was."

"Was?"

"It's tainted now. If it were daylight, I'd put a for sale sign out front right now."

"It must be hard dealing with this all on your own."

"I'll manage."

"Well, you know you could..."

"Detective Scott, right?"

"Hmm."

T.K. Richards

"Thanks for all your help tonight. I'm going to go make some calls. If you'll excuse me." Millicent stepped away into the kitchen.

Officer Reed popped back inside. "Ms. St. James, if you're ready," he said, carrying her bags to his squad car.

Chapter 2

Chariot

Walt

The officer made small talk with Millicent to get her mind off of her troubles. She barely cracked a smile at his jokes, or listened to a word he'd said until she felt the car exit off of the highway.

"Where are we going?" she asked.

"So you were ignoring me. To the station to switch cars. It was the only way the captain agreed I could offer my services. And besides, you don't want to ride to Detroit in a police car. Am I right?"

Millicent shrugged her shoulders. "Thank you for not making me sit in the back."

"That space is for criminals. You don't look like much of a criminal to me." He raised his brow.

"Normally I'd laugh at that, but due to the circumstances..."

" I understand."

"If I haven't said it before, thank you for doing this. I can pay you, or at least give you gas money for your trouble."

"That won't be necessary. I'm happy to do it. Besides, you seemed pretty shaken up back there, and I don't like seeing women in distress, or sad, or hurt, or abused. Are you positive the place I'm taking you is safe?"

"Yeah. It's my best friend's house. She's like a sister to me, and her husband is pretty cool. They always make me feel welcome. I practically have a room at their house."

"That must be nice."

The car turned into the station lot and Officer Reed opened her car door. "This will be quick. Follow me." He took her by the hand and helped her to her feet. The word about his charity spread throughout the office before they arrived. "Sit right here, Ms. St. James. I'll be right back, and we'll be on our way."

Millicent pretended not to notice the many eyes shifting in her direction, or the whispers coming from the desks surrounding her. The staff at the precinct sized her up like a piece of meat at the deli counter. Second guessing the arrangement, she repositioned herself in her seat, waiting for her officer to return from the corner where she spotted him signing paperwork.

"Reed here offered to be this pretty lady's chariot!" A loud voice shouted from behind a cubicle wall.

"She's out of your league, Reed!" said another voice from the opposite corner.

"Oh, what a knight in shining armor!" Another teased in a high pitched voice.

Reed apologized to Millicent from afar and signaled he needed one more minute. He fanned off his unit and shouted, "Pipe down! Pipe down!"

A husky officer approached Millicent. "What brings you in?" He snorted.

"I beg your pardon?"

"What's a babe like you doing in here?"

"A 'babe?'" Millicent rolled her eyes.

Officer Reed returned and picked up her bag. "Leave her alone, Jamison. She's waiting for a lift."

Derailed

"Oh yeah, where to? I can take her wherever she needs to go."

"I already offered." Officer Reed placed his hand on his belt.

"I bet you did." Jamison smiled and walked off.

"Ignore them. They don't get out much."

"Obviously."

"Let's get you to your friend's house."

They left the station nothing short of catcalls, whistles, and cheers. She lowered her head and smiled so the officer couldn't see she was amused, and erased it when he opened her door and helped her inside his classic, renovated Chevrolet Impala. "If you will, can you plug in your friend's address?" Millicent called out Landon's address into the system. "And off we go."

The hour drive felt like an interrogation. Walt hadn't realized the dry answers Millicent gave him, extended from his lack of conversational skills outside of his job.

"I feel like I'm annoying you," he said.

"You're not." Millicent's tone was less than convincing.

"That was a lie."

"Excuse me?"

"No offense. I could tell by your tone, you lied just now. I'm training to be a detective."

"Okay. Good for you, but how dare you insinuate I was lying?"

"But were you? I won't be offended by the truth."

"Okay, yes, you were annoying me with the third degree. I felt like I was still back at the precinct."

He exhaled deeply. "I'm working on that. It's my job, so I kind of can't help it at times."

"No worries."

"Now that I have you talking, and you've told me I basically suck at having a normal conversation, may I ask you something personal?"

"That depends."

" I can't place your ethnicity. What are you, if you don't mind my asking?"

"I get this question a lot."

"I'm sure. What I'm about to say isn't going to come out right, so forgive me if I do offend you, but sometimes when I am on the phone with a person I can tell if they are black or white or Spanish and so forth. Have you ever found yourself mentally visualizing what the person on the other end of a call looks like?"

Millicent chuckled. "Um, I think everyone does that."

"Well, for me and I can only speak for myself, I can even tell when I am talking to a black person that is talking white."

"What is talking white?"

He paused. "Let me try to dig myself out of this hole."

"Yeah, let's see you do that." Millicent grinned.

"I noticed you laughed a second ago."

"I did. Now dig, Officer Reed."

"Please call me Walt. Short for Walter."

"You can't dig yourself out, can you?"

"Tough crowd." He smiled. "I think the term I'm looking for is code switching. I can tell when my people are code switching— you know, talking in a tone and manner that is not their normal voice or projection."

"Nice save." Millicent smiled. "I knew what you meant. I just wanted to see you squirm."

"That's cold, Ms. St. James. You have a sense a humor. I like that."

"Are you flirting with me, Officer Reed– I mean Walt?"

"I am, Ms. St. James, who still hasn't answered my question."

Millicent stared at the officer other than an officer for the first time that night. She noticed the smoothness in his dark skin, and the fullness of his lips and felt him worthy of an answer she normally evaded.

"My family tree consists of many different backgrounds. My

grandmother was raised in the Bahamas. My grandfather was from England. He and his real family took a trip to the islands where he met my grandmother and conceived my dad in a vacant hotel room she was cleaning. My grammy never heard from my grandfather again, and the only thing she knew of him was his last name, St. James. She gave that last name to my dad, and he earned a free ride to a university here in the states. There he met and married my mother, who is mixed with everything associated with slavery and fraternizing with the Indians. And no, I don't know which tribe."

"And all of that created a world class beauty."

Millicent's cheeks flushed pink and red.

"I didn't mean to say that aloud."

Silence sat between them as the navigation system announced they were about to arrive at their destination. "I wish that drive was just a little longer," he said, parking in front of The Jeffries' house. He carried Millicent's bags to the door. "This house looks dark. Are you sure the people that live here are home?"

"It is pretty dark, but I'm sure someone's home. Landon would have told me if she were leaving town." She rang the bell.

"Who's that?" Walt pointed to a car pulling behind his in the driveway.

Millicent turned around and sucked her teeth. "Nobody."

"Whatchu doing here, Mills? And with the police no less."

Millicent turned back to Walt. "You know how you told me to ignore those people at the precinct? Do the same for him."

"Officer." Jay snickered. "You with the police? Of course you would be. What kind of trouble you got yourself into, Boughetto? I thought you were all white collar and shit. How you doing tonight overseer, I mean officer?"

"Your friend has jokes, I see." Walt muttered.

"Is this your new man, Mills?"

Walt extended his hand to Jay. "Officer Reed. And you are?"

"Talking to the lady." Jay shook his hand. "All jokes aside, Mills, you in some kind of trouble?"

"Not anymore. Where are Todd and Landon?"

"The hospital."

"Why? What happened?"

"Todd damn near burned his eyebrows off trying to outdo me on the grill. He burned his elbow pretty good, but he'll be alright. They're going to be there for a while, and you know how you and L bougie asses are. She's cold and wants a blanket, but God forbid she lays on one from the hospital."

"Well, let me in since you have the key."

Jay walked between Walt and Millicent, gave Walt a onceover, then grinned at Millicent. "Is this yours?" he asked, pointing to Millicent's bag. She nodded. "I'll take that, officer."

Walt handed the duffle to Jay as he stared at him with a curve on the side of his right lip. "You have some pretty interesting friends, Ms. St. James."

"You ain't bringing another Kevin 'round here are ya, Mills?"

"Who is Kevin?"

"No one." Millicent sighed and buried her head below her hand.

"Some clown she had taggin' along wit' her a while back."

"Kevin and I work together. Nothing more. Stop playing around, Jay."

"It was none of my business. I shouldn't have asked." Walt chuckled.

Jay grinned at Millicent. "You still haven't said why the police is dropping you off this time of night."

Millicent looked away.

"She had an intruder in her home. I offered to bring her somewhere safe."

"Get the fuck outta here. Did y'all find the person?"

Derailed

"Not yet."

"I hope you do before...Thanks for looking out for my people. Millicent ,you could have called one of us to come out there."

"I didn't mind. At all." Walt stared at Jay with his chest out. "Again, pretty interesting friends, Ms. St. James."

"I'll leave you two kids out here to say good night. I would invite you in, but I'm pretty sure my friends wouldn't like Mills entertaining some strange man in their house. Nice meeting you Officer...Reed?"

"Call me Walt."

"Ahite then, Walt."

Free from Jay's quips and intrusion, they stood on the steps clueless of what to do next. Like a teenager sneaking around behind her parents' backs, Millicent kept watch on the door, waiting for Jay to interrupt them. Walt conjured up the nerve to speak first.

"What happened to you tonight was horrible, but something good came out of it. Meeting you."

"I can't thank you enough for bringing me all the way out here. As I said before, I can pay you."

"I would never take money from a woman." He scowled. "Ms. St. James, are you seeing anyone?"

"Not at the moment. I take it you're single?"

"As a one dollar bill. Ugh, that has to be the corniest thing I have said all night."

"Yes, it is." She laughed.

"Well I'm going to get my corny ass back on the road. It was good to see that frown turn upside down."

Millicent lost the resistance to blush.

"Can I try to make you smile again— at a later date— when you feel up to it?"

"I'd like that."

Millicent watched him walk away with one foot inside of the house. She yelled, "Don't you need my number?!"

"What do you think took me so long at the precinct! I was hoping this night ended like this!"

Jay crossed Millicent's path. "Let this be the last time you bring the police to folk's house."

"Scared?"

"Never dat. You gon' be good staying here by yourself?"

"No."

"Come on and ride with me to the hospital so I can talk shit about ole copper ass."

"I'd rather you shut the hell up and just drive."

Jay opened the passenger door for Millicent. "For you, milady."

Millicent rolled her eyes and hopped in. Jay plopped in the driver's seat and revved the engine.

"What you know about cars, Mills?"

She sighed. "How to buy them and trade them in."

"Where is yours by the way?"

"Four flats in front of my house."

"Who did you piss off, girl?"

"Jay, just drive."

"How about I take L her blanket, and you come home with me? She doesn't have to know you're here. I can keep you safe tonight."

"No thank you." She scoffed.

"You'll change your mind. And when you do, holla at me."

"That won't happen."

Jay grinned. "That pig was square. Don't get too close to him."

"Why not?"

"Cuz he's gonna hate my guts when he finds out I'm the motherfucker that stole his woman from under him."

Chapter 3
New Man Who Dis
Jen

In a new bed, in a new house off the southern coast of Florida, Jen woke up to clear blue skies, and waves crashing on white sands outside her bedroom window.

"What do you call that?" Jen asked Jules, kissing her shoulder.

"That's what you call a good morning fuck that will have you thinking about me all day." He squeezed her ass until she squealed. "Good morning."

"Good morning." Jen sighed between a smile and her hair covering half her face. "What was that move you did in the end?"

"You like that, huh?"

"I did." She giggled. "You haven't done that before."

"That was just a little something something. You want me to do it again?"

"Duh." Jen laughed playfully as she and Jules wrestled on the soiled, mangled sheets beneath them. "But it will have to wait until I get home tonight."

"Listen to you. You've only been here a few months and already making me second in your life."

"Don't be like that. You know I hate being late."

"I know. It's good you like working at that spa."

"I'm doing more than working there. I'm planning to open my own spot as soon as I finish tying up loose ends with Max."

"I thought Jay was going to have full custody of him?"

"He wants to, but I can't agree to that. I'm his mother."

"And a boy needs a father."

"Are you saying you don't want Max here with us?"

"Don't put words in my mouth. What I'm saying is that as a man myself, I can honestly say I would rather my real dad be in my life instead of a substitute."

Jen sat on the edge of the bed. "I'll take that into consideration. Jay and I will do what's best for our son in the end. You had me scared for a second."

"Why?"

Looking back at Jules over her shoulder, she said, "I thought you were going to say my son wasn't wanted here. I was afraid I was going to have to leave your ass and crawl back to Detroit with egg on my face."

Jules inched closer to her and wrapped his arms around her waist. "I would never. He is a part of you. And I love every part of you. Besides, don't you think it's time you let him meet me?"

"Soon. Jay is not on board with that idea yet." She tapped the back of his hand.

"It's not like you to let him call the shots. Like you said, you are the mother after all."

Jen turned around and smirked. "Have I made a mistake?"

"What do you mean?"

"Letting you believe because you fuck me every which way even sideways you can talk shit to me."

"Whoa. Let's start this morning over." He pulled her closer. "Good morning, my long lost love."

"I need to get my day started."

Derailed

Jules followed Jen into the closet slinging clothes on the rack. He stood at the entrance and blocked her from exiting.

"I'm not letting you leave if we're on bad terms."

"We're not. But we will be if I'm late."

He moved out of her way. "Do you want my lawyer to look at your business plan?"

"No. I've got it all under control."

"I don't like when you're mad at me."

"I'm not mad."

"Then look at me."

Jen threw her clothes on the bed and faced him with her brows slightly raised higher on one side.

"Point made. I'll wait for you to cool off to ask about your plan.

"I'll tell you now. I'm opening a makeup bar. A salon dedicated to giving women makeovers, and teaching classes on how to properly apply their make-up. Not this caked-up shit all over the internet. I'll make house calls, tend to celebrities when they roll into town. That sort of thing."

"Sounds like you've done your research."

"I'm confident it can work. I envision three makeup artists and two stylists at the bar. Girls can come in and get serviced before having their pictures taken or going to prom. We'll provide self-care to women who need a day to spruce up."

Jules kissed her forehead. "You haven't opened the doors yet, and I'm already proud of you. When you finish your certification, expect a big donation from an anonymous donor."

Jen looked as if she had seen a ghost when Jules asked about her certification. He was in the dark of her flawed past and would never know her secrets, though they weighed her down. Despite her maternal attachment and hidden cries at night, she sacrificed her selfish longing to be with Max, knowing with Jay he would be heavily protected and kept safe in case anyone from her past came looking to settle the score.

Once out of the house, Jen breathed out without Jules picking her brain. She thought about her first husband, Alex, and how he ruined her ability to trust anyone, something she wished she could fully experience with Jules. He knew Jen the girl, not Jen the woman, and she had a life she could never share with him.

Jen knew he was the man for her by the way he gazed upon her when he thought she wasn't looking. His desire for her was what she longed for as he loved her in the purest form, but when she listened to her gut, the man she felt the most trustworthy with her secret was Jay. Philandering, two-timing John Jay Lloyd of all people.

Jen further questioned if being loved, and adorned, and craved would be worth it in the end, and wondered if she had been wise, or a fool for the sake of love. *'Should I have found a way to make it work with Jay? Was I weak for falling in love and thinking I could run into the arms of another man with ease? I could have followed Jay's lead and had an affair with Jules. No. Jay would have found a way to screw it up for me.'*

Thinking of Jay led her to call him. His greetings were cold in the beginning. Dry conversation. Quick hang-ups. This time he surprised her.

"Missing me yet?" He chuckled.

Jen scoffed. "How is my baby? How are you?"

"You don't have to ask that every time you call. I'm handling my business as usual."

"Of course you are, but how is my son?"

"Watch your words. 'How is *our* son?' And he is doing just fine."

"I'm coming to see him."

"The two times you have aren't enough?"

"Jay, I don't need your shit today. Okay?"

"What's wrong? Lover boy ain't living up to the hype?"

"Lover boy is perfectly fine and wants to meet Max. Are you good with that yet?"

"Nah. My boy got one daddy and one daddy only. And his mama is always welcome to come home when she's done bullshitting in the streets."

"You told me to take all the time I needed. Now you're throwing it in my face."

"Maybe I should have been clearer. I thought you would take off for a few weeks, maybe even a month. I didn't know your fling was going to result in you moving outta state."

Jen sighed. "I didn't call for a lecture."

"I might have fucked up, but did we deserve to be abandoned? You took it too far."

"What we're not going to do is blame me for our breakup."

"Our son asks me every day if you've called."

"And I do. You choose not to answer."

"I know, but I lie to him. I tell him you called while he was at soccer practice, or asleep in the car. But why do you call every day? Tell pretty boy to fuck off and come home."

"Jules is not a pretty boy."

"Whoa whoa whoa. Don't call his name to me."

"Why? Because you have never called out your coleslaw's name to me. Like Sasha."

"Who is Sasha?"

"It's been that many? You can't remember their names?" Jen sucked her teeth. "You haven't changed one bit."

"Whether you believe it or not, some things have changed."

"Like what?"

"Things," Jay muttered.

Jen took a play from Jay's book and abruptly ended their call. He dialed her back. She swiped her phone and sent him to voicemail faster than a person scrolling past the pictures they weren't given permission to see.

She called Landon. "Who is the new bimbo?"

Landon coughed. "Good morning to you too. How is the sunshine state?"

"Hot. Now fill me in. Have you met her yet?"

"I have not. And Todd hasn't mentioned anything to me. I've been around pretty heavy, filling in your shoes until you come back. When will that be?"

"I don't think I could come back if I wanted to."

"Why do you say that?"

"Because I could tell in Jay's voice that he is about done with me as I am him."

"Men don't pine away for a woman that long. My uncle got himself a new wife in less than a month when my aunt died."

"They really are pieces of shit, aren't they?"

"Facts. And this is Jay we're talking about. What did you expect?"

Jen hit the steering wheel and pulled over to the side of the road. "Hold please." She screamed with the phone pressed to her chest.

"I heard that. Do this. Close your eyes and tell me who do you see yourself with?"

"Jules."

"Do you feel anything other than hate for Jay?"

"I don't hate Jay. I'm disappointed in us. He hurt me and humiliated me, but I do like how he used to beg for me to come home. He didn't do that today."

"Jen, if you come back Jay will continue to be who you know him to be, and you will regret losing the man who obviously truly loves you."

"I guess I just needed to hear that from the wisest person I know."

"You should come home this weekend. Stay with me. It'll be fun. Millicent is already here, so we can make it a girls' margarita weekend or something."

"Why is Millicent there?"

"She's been living here for a few weeks now. Someone vandalized her place, and she's too scared to live alone at the moment."

"That person really did a number on her. Now I understand why she hasn't given me an update on how long I have to collect that money in Sweden. Give her my best, will ya? Better yet, I'll do it myself this weekend. I'm coming to see my boy. But the girls' night will have to wait. I'm not coming alone."

Chapter 4

The Outsider

Landon

Landon's party for Jen turned out to be a disaster before it got started, thanks to Todd inviting Jay, and his son Ephram, without clearing it with her first. His apology for doing so was not received on her behalf, therefore setting the tone for the party.

Jay showed up in rare form. Flamboyant and cockier than ever. He pulled a page from The Book of Nas in his attire. Casual black chinos and matching blazer above a black label tee and medium gold link chain shining from his neck, with fresh white sneakers with fat laces. Landon gave him the side eye when he arrived.

"Now you know Jen is coming home to see her baby. Why would you agree to come tonight instead of being at home so Max could enjoy seeing both of you getting along?"

"He likes going to Mrs. Latham's house. I told her Jen was coming to pick him up."

"Did you tell Jen that?"

"I'll tell her when she gets here."

"Jay, I want you to know I'm biting my tongue. Okay?"

"Ey, I ain't the one who left. Don't be mad you got stuck with the realest in the breakup. Let me kiss the host." He puckered his lips. "Where is T?"

"Boy, come in and go out back."

"If you need me to make sure he doesn't burn those thick ass eyebrows, just say that."

Landon took a deep breath, then hurried into the kitchen to lay out the food while eavesdropping on the conversation between the men. Millicent popped in.

"You need some help?"

"Yeah. Grab that pan and meet me outside. I'm trying to listen in on what the boys are talking about. Jen thinks Jay is seeing someone. I'm trying to find out before she gets here."

"Did her and Jules break up or something?"

"No. But she said she can tell he's into someone. Come on and help me listen in."

Millicent pretended not to notice the look Jay gave her when she walked outside. She recognized he was undressing her with his eyes, and it puzzled her that she liked it.

"What time did you tell Mr. Officer to drop by?" Landon asked her.

"Eight o'clock."

Jay blew from his nose loud enough for Millicent to hear him.

"I can't wait to meet him." Landon squealed and rolled her shoulders.

"Todd, did you know these two invited the po-po to your house?"

Landon cut him off. "Jay, I need you to simmer down. The party hasn't started yet, and you are already starting shit. Todd, check him please."

Jay clicked his teeth, glancing at Millicent with a seductive eye. She followed Landon back inside, blushing with her head hung low, guilty of playing phone tag with both Jay and Walt.

Derailed

The doorbell rang. "I'll get it." Millicent sprang for the door. "Oh, it's you guys," she said to McCaine, Tammy, Brian and Kim.

"Well, hey to you too." Tammy narrowed her eyes and passed her a bottle of wine. "You're looking well, given what you've been through."

"I didn't mean to offend you guys. I just thought you were my plus one. Everybody's out back."

"Is Jen here yet?"

"We're waiting on her too."

Landon greeted her guests and followed everyone to the deck. Todd swiped a kiss from her as she brought out the final dish. "Everyone can eat," she announced over the music, shaking on the top step. Todd returned and lowered the sound of 90's hip hop playing over the radio and gained everyone's attention.

"Everybody, Landon and I have two special guests tonight. I want you all to meet my son, Ephram."

The shocked faces of their guests had a hard time settling on who to look at, the boy or Landon. He stood next to Todd, looking at the adults with big dough eyes, twisting from side to side. Landon created a space between her and Todd, red faced with a fake smile on her lips and a stiff forehead.

"He's a cutie," said Tammy, coaching Landon to relax with muttered lip movement.

Millicent whispered, "We may have to drag her off of that step. She looks like a mannequin up there."

"I've never seen someone blink so much," Kim added.

"Come over here, baby. You hungry? You want me to fix you a plate?"

"No. I wanna go back in the house and play my video game," he said, looking up at Todd.

Todd smiled down at him. "That's cool. I just wanted you to meet your family. These people are always going to be around, so get to know them. Okay?"

He nodded his head, then repeated himself. "Can I go play my game now?"

"Yeah. Go 'head." Todd rubbed the top of his head.

He ran off, and Todd inched closer to Landon. "See, that wasn't so bad. Was it?"

"I think Jen may be at the door. I'll be right back."

She went inside and leaned back against the door, holding her hands to her chest and exhaling in short breaths. Todd turned the music back on as Jen's silhouette formed at the door. Landon opened it before she rang the bell. "It's so good to have you home." She and Jen hugged.

"I missed you," Jen whispered in her ear. "You know Jules."

"Nice seeing you again. How did she manage to sneak you away?"

"I'm actually flying out on the redeye."

"Yeah, he can't be away from the team right now. I just wanted him to meet Max. Even if it was for a hot minute."

"How did that go?" Landon asked under her breath.

"It went. Jay wasn't happy about it, but he held his composure in front of our boy so...cool points to him, I guess."

Landon bit her bottom lip. "Ha. That explains it."

"What?"

"He's in rare form tonight."

"Shit. Well, Jules and I are only staying for like an hour. I have to drop him off at the airport, and I promised Max I would pick him up and let him sleep at the hotel tonight so he can get in the pool tomorrow. I hope you won't be mad?"

"Jen, with the way the night is going, I might kick everyone out after you leave."

"What happened?"

"We'll talk later. Jules, let's go make you feel awkward and introduce you to the boys. Mine won't bite, but Jay..."

"I expect nothing less from him after meeting him earlier

today." He laughed.

A record might as well have scratched when Landon walked through her patio doors with Jen and Jules on her heels. Jay turned up his lip and snickered with Todd. Landon narrowed her eyes at her husband, and summoned him to her side. "The chain is pulling her ball. You better go before you get sent to bed with no dinner." Jay chuckled and gave him dap. Todd placed his hand in the small of Landon's back as she formally introduced him to Jules.

"You taking care of my people?" Todd and Jules pounded fists.

"It's been my pleasure."

Millicent walked over. "Good to see you, Julian."

"I told you, my friends call me Jules. And it's good to see you too. Mal's been asking about you."

"Tell him I'm cool."

"Landon told me what happened. Did they ever find the guy?"

"Nope. Not one lead, but I don't want to talk about that tonight. I've put it behind me, put my house up for sale, traded in my car, and am moving on. But we'll catch up on all of that tomorrow at brunch, right?"

"Fah sho."

"I'll be right back. I think my date finally arrived. Look at me. I'm no longer the fifth wheel. Excuse me."

Landon tapped her arm. "I'll join you. I need to check on Todd's son."

"Wait. He's here?" Jen asked.

"Yeah. I'll bring him out so you can meet him."

Millicent looked through the blinds from the front room. Landon comforted her. "I'm sure he'll be here. Go hang out. I'll keep watch." She raced off to Todd's man cave. The television had animated army men on the screen, turned up loud as the music outside. "Ephram!" she called. No answer. She checked the kitchen, sure he decided to finally eat. It was empty. She sped down the hall and gasped.

"Get down from there before you fall and break your neck," she warned him, sitting on the edge of the banister.

"What would you do if I fall?"

"What? I'd call 911. Now get down!"

"I would tell the police you pushed me."

"What did you say?"

"You heard me."

"Get your little ass down from there right now!"

Landon watched him climb back over the banister and sent him to his room. The room Todd was thrilled to paint blue and decorate with sports decals, shelves of balls from golf to basketball, and pictures of the local legends. She pulled Todd away from Jay, sending heat signals to Jules's back.

"Didn't take you long to escape Jules, I see."

"You mean Julian? His friends call him Jules." Todd and Jay chuckled.

"You two are so childish."

"He hit it off with Brian and McCaine pretty good. You know. Talking that college shit."

"I need you inside. We have a problem," she exclaimed in a whisper and repeated what Ephram said to her.

"You must have heard him wrong," Todd replied.

"Todd, I know what I heard, and he has to go home."

"Landon calm down. The boy just got here."

"And he threatened to lie about me to the police. The cops and the media will take a child's word over an adult's word at the drop of a dime! And they wouldn't care that he's lying. I have too much to lose over this ridiculousness!" Landon exclaimed.

"Where is he?"

"In your cave. I'll go pack his belongings."

Derailed

Todd found Ephram playing his game. He sat next to him and picked up the extra remote. "I used to be pretty good at these things. Let's see if I still have it," he said, working his way in. "Are you hungry yet?"

"I ate some of those chips Ms. Landon put on the counter."

"We have more than chips out back. How about I fix you a plate after I beat you one round?"

"No thanks."

"Say, did you say something to Landon to upset her?"

"No."

"You sure? She says she asked you to not sit on the railing upstairs. She was scared you would hurt yourself. Did you say you would tell the police she pushed you if you fell."

"I didn't say that."

"Okay. Do you remember what you said?"

"I haven't said anything to her."

Todd paused the game with his remote. "Stop playing for a second. Ephram, look at me and tell me the truth. What did you say? Landon wouldn't make something up like that, Son."

"I thought you would be on my side."

"On your side for what? You said nothing happened."

Ephram sighed.

"Come on. I'm going to take you home. We'll try this another time." Todd's voice cracked.

Landon walked in with Ephram's bags. Her chest was tight and her back stiff from the stress she predicted when news of Ephram ruined her happiness. She watched Todd from behind, feeling the hurt he released in the room. "I'm going to leave these here. It was nice to have you spend the day with us, Ephram." Landon dropped the bags and rejoined her guests outside, intruding on a conversation between McCaine, Tammy, and Jay, entertaining the comedic couple of the group with all of the nicknames he created for Jules.

"I guess the police ain't showing up tonight, L. It's probably for the best. This party went down the moment Rick Fox dropped in. Where my boy T at?"

Landon stumbled on her words with a lie on the tip of her tongue, and a tear forming in the corner of her eye. Tammy read her body language and noticed the water bubbling above her lower lash. "Something's wrong." She scowled, nudging Landon to a private corner.

Landon nervously shook her head. "It's happening. Just like I said it would." She sniffed and wiped the tear. "Don't mind me. I'm just a little upset. Todd has to leave and take his son home."

"Now?"

Landon nodded. "You won't believe what happened in the house."

"Remember I've been here before. Try me," said Tammy.

The friends noticed Landon wiping tears and gathered around. With shaky breaks she retold what transpired in the house.

Tammy's mouth dropped. "I was hoping you were wrong. Secretly I wished this would be an experience you'd actually enjoy."

"I tried. I don't know what more I can do. And in every outcome, I am the bad guy, but how can I trust being around a kid who would say something like that?"

"Todd has himself in deep shit with this one." McCaine blew from his mouth.

"That boy wouldn't set foot back in my house," Kim added.

"I was thinking the same thing. The law will make an example out of innocent people when it comes to children." Brian sighed.

Millicent interrupted. "If he would say something like that, do you think he would steal? Never mind. Excuse me. I need to check my room."

Chapter 5

Who You Wit'

Jay

J ay's eyes followed Millicent running into the house, tuning out the group sympathizing with Landon. He chimed in, "L, that's messed up what the little boy said, but it doesn't change the fact Todd is his daddy. Give little man time to adjust. He's been over here how many times. Two? Three?"

"Jay, you hate the police more than anyone I know. How would you honestly feel if a kid threatened to have you arrested for absolutely nothing."

"He was just talking. He wasn't gonna do that, L. He was just being a kid."

"Well, let him be a kid over at your house."

"Um. No." Jen interrupted. "I don't need him influencing my sweet boy."

"So just like that, the kid has been alienated," said Jay, looking around at everyone. "If y'all will excuse me."

Landon pointed at Jay walking up the stairs. "See. I'm the bad guy no matter what. I knew this shit would happen."

Jay went inside and sought out Millicent. He posed in the

entrance of her room door with a grin on the side of his lips. Millicent, busy fumbling through her bags counting credit cards and jewelry, didn't feel his presence as he gawked at her curves.

"Is anything missing?" He propped himself against the door.

Millicent gasped and held her chest. "You scared me. And no, it looks like everything is still here."

"Good. That kid has everyone outside in a tizzy. I would hate for them to add thief to his name."

"What are you doing up here?"

"Checking up on what's soon to be mine. Especially since the overseer is a no show. But that's good for me."

"The night's not over."

"It is for him. Stop frontin, Mills. You probably read my texts over and over at night, wishing I was here keeping you company."

"You're really doing this with Jen downstairs?"

"Jen has moved on, and so have I."

Millicent studied Jay with a close eye. She did enjoy reading his texts, and thought of how one in particular made her believe he truly was into her.

"In one of your messages, you said you knew this would happen."

"Like you didn't."

"Jay, what do you want with me?"

"You already know." He moved closer.

"Nothing about you and me makes sense."

"That doesn't mean it wouldn't be right. And I bet it feels right too." Jay touched her skin for the first time, tracing the curve below her cheek.

Millicent shivered. "I am smarter than this."

"That might be your problem. You think too much. That's why you don't have a man. Take a chance for once. I swear you won't regret it."

"I don't want to hurt my best friend."

Derailed

"How can you when she doesn't feel anything for me anymore. She's made her choice and she's happy. Don't you deserve to be happy too?" He stunned her with a kiss to her lips. "Tell me you didn't feel that."

Millicent looked into his eyes and didn't answer. Jay stole a second kiss, this time with his eyes open. "How have I not noticed you before now?" he said, and took her in his arms, taming his dominant beast within. Millicent brought out a sensual side in him. He wasn't what she was used to, and he acted according to her needs, hypnotized by the softness of her skin blessing his fingertips. Passion he didn't know existed flowed through him, causing him to see Millicent more than the dollar store fucks, or corner girl quick jobs he was used to. She wasn't to be played with or fucked in that moment. She needed to be made love to.

The way Jay held her close, gently kissing her lips and giving her body the attention it craved surprised her. This wasn't the Jay she had come to know over the years. The Jay who bigoted his way through neighborhoods of women. The Jay who taunted her for calling him on his bullshit. This was a man who seduced her with charm and wit, successfully convincing her to go against what she knew was wrong, and made it feel right.

Millicent surrendered her body to her longtime adversary, giving him control of it to do as he pleased. She weakened from his strong hands and allowed him to lift her legs into the crease of his elbows, and place her pussy on the hard knot tightened against his zipper

"That's all you," he said. "You ready to let me taste?"

She nodded.

Jay laid her on the bed, pressing his trapped dick against her with pressure until she squirmed. He smiled. "I know it's wet." He pecked her lips, creating a trail towards her neck. Her gasps for air excited him more than when she played hard to get, and he rose above her for another look of his latest dream turning into reality.

Over the past few weeks, he imagined how this moment would be— him pounding on her from the rear and pulling her long wavy hair towards him while arching her back like the letter C. But he couldn't handle her that way once the moment arrived.

"What is it?" she asked.

He puckered his lips. "Show me you want me."

Millicent's legs spread eagle. She removed her panties and threw them at his face. Jay caught them and placed them in his mouth.

"This better not be some sort of game, Jay," she said.

Jay freed his mouth and dropped to his knees. "Let me clean up your mess."

His breath against her throbbing flesh and admired its beauty with his fingers. Tracing her entrance like a delicate flower before licking her center. His tongue tasted the nectar dripping from her folds and he moaned. "This pretty pussy hasn't been tended to."

He kissed it with a long steady motion from the bottom to the top. Millicent mangled the covers in her hands. Jay thrashed his tongue against her shaking body hard, counting how many times her ass jiggled in his face. "Yes, Jay. Just like that. Keep doing it just like that," she groaned. He shocked her with fast soft licks and a full mouthed kiss to her quivering pussy. The aggressive tongue stabs and repetitive, soft pecks to her slit made her stomach cave as she erupted in his mouth.

Her hands cradled his head tight to her hole, restricting him from breathing, and the intensity of her orgasm shook the bed and his soul. He was ready to plow.

Jay rose to his feet, reached in his wallet, and covered himself while Millicent squirmed and held herself on the bed. Seeing him protect them made her think of the stories Jen shared of finding condoms they never used. She respected him for it, but also questioned herself. *'This is a mistake. What the fuck am I doing with him?'*

Jay wiped his mouth with her panties, slid between her legs where they once covered her, and positioned himself to enter her world. Millicent contemplated telling him she'd changed her mind, but feeling his very grown manliness against her aching womb clouded her judgment. She wanted it. Needed it.

Slowly he danced his way inside of her, holding back the fast paced assault he imagined he'd do to her in his dreams. He *grinded* his cock hard and slow into her corners, listening to her breathe sighs of relief. Millicent's nails sunk into his back.

"Scratch me, baby, I don't care," he whispered, digging harder and deeper in her zone. "You like that?"

"Yes, Jay, yes."

"Say my name again."

"Yes, Jay." Millicent panted in his ear.

He cuffed both of her thighs from the back and brought them forward. The faster their hearts beat, the weaker Jay's elated mind could no longer tame his beast. "Can I go deeper, baby?" he asked, doing so without her permission.

"Mmm hmm," she answered, clenching her walls around him so tight he nearly burst early.

"What is mmm hmm? I wanna hear yes Jay. I like how you sound when you say my name."

"Yes Jay. Go deeper." Millicent thrust her hips forward.

Jay lowered his torso and kissed her. "You want everybody to hear you outside?"

"I don't care," she whispered.

Jay grinned and kissed her to silence the pleasure escaping her lips.

Chapter 6

A Woman & Her Intuition

Jen

The dilemma between Landon and Todd killed the mood of the party. Jen shifted the attention to herself and lied, "Jules and I decided Max would love to see the planes take off at night. We're going to get him and call it night. Are we still on for brunch tomorrow?" Landon hugged her. Jen turned to Jules. "I'm going to go tell Millicent bye and visit the ladies' room. Meet you in the car."

Jen freshened up in the downstairs guest bathroom. Faint whispers and moans traveled through the vent. As she continued to primp in the mirror, the sounds grew louder and familiar. She stepped out and turned towards the stairwell, doubting herself as she climbed. The sound of Jay's voice grew stronger behind the door in Millicent's room.

Her eyes widened after cracking a thin opening. Jay stood behind Millicent, his body draped around hers, kissing her neck as she giggled and swayed in his arms.

She closed the door shut, dashed down the stairs, and went back into the bathroom. She stared at herself forming tears in the mirror, questioning her feelings and reaction to what she saw. After tiring of looking at herself, she rested her back against the door. One tear fell. She wiped it from her cheek, took another glimpse of herself in the mirror, and consoled her reflection. "That's all they get."

Frozen from the betrayal, thoughts of the times they all spent together flashed in her mind. She wondered if she had missed something over the years. Had she missed a flirtation between them, or signs they shared a connection? She came up empty.

A knock at the door broke her trance.

"Jen, are you alright?" Jules asked.

She opened the door. "Yeah. You ready to go?"

"Been ready. There's a guy outside asking where he should park."

Jen scoffed as he rang the doorbell.

"You sure you okay? You seem upset. Did Jay say something to you?"

"I'm fine. Really. Let's get out of here."

Walt stood at the door with flowers and a bottle of wine. Nervously he smiled. "You must be Todd and Landon."

"No," Jen replied sharply.

Jules scowled at her tone. "They are in the back. Julian." His hand reached forward.

"Walter," he replied, shaking Jules's hand.

"And this is Jen."

"You must be Millicent's date. She's been waiting on you to arrive. Nice to finally meet you. We were actually on our way out, but please come in. Everyone is on the deck. Just go right through those doors." Jen pointed past the kitchen.

"Nice meeting you."

As Jen and Jules finagled their way between the cars parked in the yard, Jay stepped onto the porch with his phone to his ear. Jen's face turned red. "Do you need me to drive?"

Derailed

Jules huffed. "Something definitely happened. You're acting strange out of the blue."

"Now is not the time. Just get me out of here. Please," she begged as Todd pulled up behind them.

He waved to them leaving, receiving a cold stare and cut eyes as the car drove away. Jay met him in the driveway, smoking a joint.

"What's with them?" Todd asked Jay.

"With who?"

"Jen and Miami Beat."

Jay laughed. "That was probably my best name for him, ain't it? Shit, I don't know. I haven't said a word to either of them. You got problems of your own from what I hear. Your ole lady's out back crying. You got your hands full, T." Jay passed the joint to Todd.

"Don't I know it." He inhaled a long toke.

"You think he said it?"

"Yup."

"Whatchu gon' do?"

"Shit if I know." He exhaled. "Let me go check on my wife. This is gonna be a long ass night."

"If you need some privacy, send Mills over to my house. I got a special place for her." Jay smirked.

"Shut up man." Todd laughed.

Their joking ceased immediately as they walked out to the deck. Todd's eyes rested on Landon's red face, and Jay's eyes widened at the sight of Millicent sitting next to Walt holding a bouquet of flowers in her hand. He whispered to Todd, "That's the po-po."

Todd looked over to Millicent. "Is this your friend who can't tell time?"

Walt stood up. "Sorry for being late. In my line of work, you never know when someone decides to do something stupid and force you to put in overtime."

"I'm just fucking with you. Todd. Glad you could make it." He offered a shake of hands..

"Walter Reed. And this is..." Walt's eyes shifted to Jay as his inquiry lingered.

"Jay. We met the other night." He grinned. "I see you found your way back."

"That I did."

"Well, enjoy what's left of the party. As for me it's over. Be easy, man."

Todd made his way over to Landon. He held her at the waist, waiting for a moment to interrupt Brian telling one of his long-winded stories. "I'm going to steal my wife away for a minute." He pulled her aside, surveying every eye upon them. "So everyone knows what happened, and you've been crying. You know I don't like seeing you sad." He kissed her cheek.

"How did it go?"

"He finally admitted that he said it."

"Did he say why?"

"No, but let's talk about it later. Right now I want to dance with my wife, get drunk, and send these people home."

"We could send them home now. Both guests of honor have left so..."

Todd laughed. "And so has Jay."

"Don't get me started on him."

"What did the homie do now to piss you off."

Landon pulled back from Todd. "Read this text from Jen."

Todd guffawed with a smile fighting for a place on the sides of his mouth. "Yo! That motherfucker!" he exclaimed in a whisper.

Landon took the joke further. "More like friend fucker."

Todd laughed hysterically and glanced at Millicent sitting with Walt on the back porch. She looked like a deer trapped in headlights, bored out of her mind as the cop yapped his gums endlessly. Todd pulled Landon close, chuckling in her ear. "Yeah, it's time to send everyone home."

Chapter 7

It's a No For Me
Millicent

One by one, they rid the house of their guests, with Walt and Millicent as the exception. For at least an hour, Todd and Landon sat with them listening to music, and listening to Walt tell them about the high speed car chase that nearly killed him before he made it to the party.

Todd took more of an interest in him than he did Jules. Landon loved when he engaged with others besides Jay, showing an interest in new avenues and personalities.

"We should get together and go out on a double date one night." Landon suggested.

Todd caught Millicent sneaking a dirty look her way and laughed to himself.

"Sounds good to me. I'll wait on Millicent here to tell me when's a good time, and hope to make it happen. And on that note, I better get going. It's been a hell of a day, but I wouldn't dare keep this young lady hanging on a string. I had a good time tonight. Lovely meeting you two."

"Let me show you out." Millicent hopped to her feet.

The sky was black above them, and so was Millicent's heart,

dragging her feet to come clean with Walt waiting for a kiss good night.

"I need to tell you something," she said.

"I can tell there is someone else."

"Huh? No. Um. I put my house up for sale. I'm not coming back to Toledo. I've been offered a job and will move out of my friend's house once my place is out of escrow."

"Sounds like you're saying we should quit while we're ahead."

Millicent took a deep breath and bit her fingernails.

"I respect you letting me down easy. But what was with the texts you've been sending me?"

"I do like you. It's just not the right time. I hope you understand?"

Walt sighed. "I would understand if you allowed me to take you out on a proper date. One where I'm not late. And if you want to write me off after that, I'll bow out of the running."

Millicent blushed. "And when do you propose we go on this date?"

"How's tomorrow? I'll settle for a late lunch date to not put any pressure on you."

"You would drive all the way home tonight, and back here again tomorrow just to take me out?"

"Pick you up at three." Walt kissed the back of her hand and left.

Millicent followed the sound of dishes clanking in the kitchen. Landon stopped wrapping food with foil and loading the dishwasher, and stared at her, hoping she'd crack.

"He's good for you." Landon led to kill the silence between them. "You won't find another good one like him is all I'm saying. He's a good catch. He's handsome, well-mannered, polite, attentive, a conversationalist with an actual job this time. When was the last time a man brought you flowers?"

"I don't know."

"And excuse me for saying, but I can tell he has a nice body. Those broad shoulders on that smooth chocolate skin, and bald head." Landon sucked her teeth. "You are crazy to let him slip through your fingers. I'm trying to understand why you aren't in the car going home with him tonight. He was practically begging you to like him with those slanted smoldering eyes."

"We have brunch tomorrow."

"Girl, fuck brunch. A fine ass man drove out of his way to see you to safety, came to meet your friends, brought you flowers and the host a bottle of wine. What do you want?"

"Chemistry. I want chemistry. Hell, you felt more for him than I did. Do you want his number?"

"I'll take it if Todd doesn't get his shit together."

"Girl, please. Todd is crazy about you, and you ain't going nowhere. You two are just going through a rough patch."

Landon sighed. "Nice try. We're talking about you."

Millicent laughed off Landon's attempt to steer the conversation. The buzzing of her cell phone silenced the both of them and they stared at each with guilt ridden eyes.

Jay: You still over there entertaining five-o?

No: Millicent

Jay: Are you sliding through or am I gonna have to kidnap you?

Let me think on it: Millicent

Jay: Quit playing. Your mind is already made up.

Cocky much?: Millicent

Jay: I'm trying to☺

After watching Millicent with a close eye, Landon pried. "You've got that look. What did he say?" Millicent continued to text and ignored her question. Landon stopped talking. She looked on as Millicent typed a mile a minute, blushing and smiling every time she pressed send..

"You were saying?" Millicent asked Landon.

"Who is that?"

"I'm sorry, why is this conversation so weird?" Millicent frowned.

"I'm trying to see where your head is."

The phone buzzed again.

Jay: I'm ready to see you now. #unfinishedbusiness

Millicent blurted, "Landon, I think you and Todd could use some privacy tonight after what happened today. I'll be back in time for brunch tomorrow."

"Where are you staying?" Landon giggled.

"I don't follow."

"Toledo or Jay's house?"

The look of a stuck deer returned to her face. Landon packed the foil covered dishes into the fridge, laughing like a movie villain. "So Jay fucks that good huh?" Her laugh grew louder and insulting.

"How do you know?" Millicent whispered.

"Why are you whispering? Todd knows what y'all did in the upstairs of his house."

"But how?"

"Jen saw you."

"Oh fuck. I'm not coming to brunch tomorrow."

"Yeah, if I were you I probably wouldn't."

"How the hell did this happen? You two have hated each other for so long."

"Landon, it was so intense. I have no idea how we got here. I agreed to go over his house and talk about it."

"You must think I'm slow. Ain't no talking happening over there tonight." Landon snickered.

"Jen hates me, doesn't she?"

Landon shrugged. "I don't know. If she does, you can't blame her."

"I have been pushing Jay away for weeks. I told him I didn't want to hurt Jen, but he refused to let up."

"Because he's Jay. He's used to getting what he wants."

"So what should I do?"

"The safest choice is Walt, but you're grown. Do what you want. Technically, you already have. So..."

Millicent stared at the latest message on her phone. She exhaled deeply and typed her reply as Landon shamed her with whimsical eyes.

"Don't wait up."

Chapter 8

The Straw

Landon

The sink was clear, the counters wiped, and the final light switched off for the night. The hours she spent avoiding her husband were hours he spent waiting for her to come to bed, and a looming conversation of the mishap they dreaded, but needed to have.

Landon climbed in bed, sighed, and turned her back to her husband. He sat up against the headrest, shirtless and bright-eyed.

"This is the first time in weeks we've had the house to ourselves, and this is how we're going to spend it?"

"I thought you were sleep."

"I waited up for you." Todd stared at her back, waiting for her to face him.

She didn't budge. "You know I can't go to bed with dishes in the sink. And after Millicent left, Jen canceled brunch. I figured I should tackle everything tonight so I can sleep in and relax tomorrow. Good night."

"Landon, you know damn well we can't go to bed like this."

"I know we shouldn't, but I was hoping after we came

together to get everyone out of here tonight, we could just go with that and call it a night. I'm tired."

"Landon, the boy is my son. I can't send him home every time he does something you don't like."

She rolled her body and faced him. "Is that what his mother said to you?"

"No, that's me telling you that I'm not doing that again. I only did it tonight because we had a house full of people. But don't ask me to do that again."

Landon sat up in the bed and looked straight ahead. She replayed Todd's words, mouthing them to herself over and over until she worked herself into a tizzy.

She stared at him as if he had stolen money from her purse. "Don't ask– you– to make me feel comfortable in my own house? Don't ask –you– to have my back, like you've been asking me to have yours? And don't bring light to what threatens me– if your son is involved? Did I hear that correctly?"

"I didn't say..."

"Not in those words, but it's the same thing. You know, against my wishes and better judgment, I went along with this because you promised everything was going to be fine. For you, I stayed. I put in effort. And what do I get? A pre-meditated threat from a child that could ruin me, and his daddy telling me how shit is going to be no matter what."

"I didn't say..."

"But you did. Just not in those words. How can you not see what he said is no laughing matter? This shit is serious, and you're instructing me to take it lightly."

"I had a talk with him. He doesn't know why he said it, but I'm going to work with him so he doesn't do anything to make you not want to be around him."

"Work with him where? Here?" Landon raised her voice.

"So you're back on that?"

"I am." Landon took a breath. "I don't hate the boy, but I don't trust him after tonight. I need to tread carefully around him. I can't make where I stand any clearer. I hope you get that. And again, good night. Love you."

Landon turned her back to Todd a second time and drifted off to sleep with ease. He sat on the edge of the bed, cradling his head between his legs as his feet tapped the top of his leather slippers below the foot board.

In the morning, Landon reached over to Todd's side of the bed. She opened her eyes when cold sheets stunned her fingertips and groaned. "And so it begins." She threw on lounge wear to put on a pot of coffee, fixing Todd's the way he liked, one cream, one sugar, and added a hack his family swore by– a pinch of salt. She strolled into his man cave. The television was off, the bar light was blacked, and the blanket resting on the corner of the sofa was still folded with the creases and tucked triangles on the edges. She checked the backyard. No Todd. She peeped through the shutters, assuming she would catch a glimpse of him finally cutting the branches that were scratching against the living room windows. Still no sign of Todd. Her face turned to stone when she made her way to the garage and saw his car was gone, and the reality of their new chapter crept in their house without a grace period, or manual on how to navigate through the troubled waters drowning them.

Chapter 9

House of Whores

Jen

Jen's hidden rage didn't fool Jules. He missed his flight, concerned he was on the verge of losing her a second time. With Max spending the night, he checked into the room next door. "Let's eat breakfast downstairs. You, me, and little man," he suggested, standing outside what was his room the night before.

"I canceled brunch with the girls, so that works." She looked over her shoulder before giving Jules a kiss good night.

"And you're sure you're alright?" he hounded her.

The light in her eyes dimmed. "I'll tell you about it tomorrow. I need to sleep on it before speaking on how I feel at the moment."

"Just tell me. Is it me?"

"It's not you. You've been great."

Jules exhaled and snuck a quick peck to her lips.

In the morning, he surprised Jen and Max wearing his swim shorts to breakfast. "Somebody wanted to go swimming today, right?" Max jumped up and down pulling off his pajamas.

"Thank you," Millicent mouthed.

"I couldn't sleep much, so I ordered room service last night. It was nothing to brag about. After the pool, I'm taking you two to lunch. Wherever you want to go."

"It'll be just you and me. Max has been invited to a birthday party at one o'clock."

"I better impress him in the water then."

To Jules, Jen seemed more like herself sitting by the pool watching him lose swim races to Max. As the love of Jen's life warmed up to him, he saw a life with them both in Miami.

On the way back to their rooms, he whispered in her ear as Max ran ahead of them down the hall. "You can't be without him. Bring him to live with us."

"I will have a battle on my hands to do so. It would have to be shared custody."

"Have you asked?"

"I will, but I know who and what I'm up against."

On the way to the birthday party, Jen asked Max if he would like to leave Detroit and move with her to Miami.

"Is Daddy coming too?"

"No, baby. You and I will live with Julian."

"I want Daddy to come too."

"He will visit you whenever you want."

Max frowned. "When are you moving back in our house?"

Jen felt a sharp pain in her chest. Knots formed around her heart, and she teared up behind her sunglasses. "Look, Mrs. Latham is already here to watch you at the party. Mommy has to go see Mrs. Landon for a second. But I promise I'll be right back to pick you up. Go have fun."

Jules saw Jen wipe the second tear dripping below her lens. "I'll take him over to her," he offered.

She looked away from them and stared at herself in the side

view mirror. Caught in a daze, she missed Mrs. Latham and Max waving goodbye to her as Jules raced back to the car.

"Jen, I can't stay in the dark much longer. What has you so upset?"

"Plug in this address," she said.

"That's not an answer."

"I'm about to show you what's bothering me."

She entered her old home and exhaled a deep breath at the scent of loud vanilla musk diffusing from the plug at the entrance. "This place hasn't been dusted in weeks," she mumbled, tapping her heels across the hardwood floor in the living room. Jay burst from the back of the house— dick slinging with his gun cocked pointing at Jen. She sat on the couch. "Put that away." She fanned him off.

"What the fuck are you doing in here? Where's my boy?" He placed the safety on the gun and hid it behind his back.

"Birthday party. Whose car is out front?"

"You don't live here no more, Jen."

"Did she tell you I know?"

Jay covered his penis with his free hand. "Yeah. She told me."

"Tell her to come out."

"Jen. Why are you here?"

"I'm testing myself."

"I think it's best if you come back later on so we can talk about this. I'on want no drama at my house, Jen. You know what's up."

"I do." She shook her head. "How long?"

Jay sighed and locked eyes with her. "A day."

"You expect me to believe that?"

"I don't have a reason to lie."

"Never behind my back?" Jen raised her brow.

"Now I've down some stupid shit, but I wouldn't do you like that. Neither would she."

"How did it happen?"

"Damn, Jen! Come on!" Jay shuddered.

"You know I know where the guns are hidden." Jen pointed a gun made with her thumb and index finger at Jay. "Bloooow! Right in the pinga. The thing you've tricked to death."

"The fuck, Jen." Jay softened his tone. "I'm to blame. I went after her when she moved in with L. She gave me the cold shoulder until yesterday. It just happened."

"You love her?"

Jay stuttered. "Th-th-this just started last night Jen!"

Jen shook her head and scoffed. Her scoff morphed into an inaudible whispering monologue, followed by an uncontrollable snicker. Jay looked over his shoulder and eyed Millicent peeping through a crack from his bedroom door.

Jen's chuckles stopped. "I could tell the last time we talked you were falling for someone, but damn, I didn't expect this." She rose from the couch. "What is with you? Do you get off by doing fucked up shit to me? Were my feelings a game to you?"

"I can never make up all the wrong I've done to you. I took care of you, but I know that wasn't enough."

"Loyalty is all I wanted."

"I know that. But don't act like you didn't leave me for that pretty motherfucker when I was trying to make things right between us."

"You are full of jokes. Making things right by fucking my friend." Jen sucked her teeth. "I have the answer I was looking for. I don't care. I'm not losing anything here. You were never going to be what I needed." Jen smiled. "And lawyer up. I'm coming back for my boy. If you still want to be in his life, we can set up visitation, but he's coming with me."

"I'll see you in court."

Jen grinned. "He's all I have, and I will not lose. And I'd kill you if I did."

Derailed

"She means it, Jay. Don't push her." Millicent's voice echoed down the hall.

"You might want to listen to your new fuck buddy."

Chapter 10

Every Girl Has A Secret
Millicent

Jen strolled out of the house that used to be hers and left the door open. Jay secured the house and told Millicent it was safe to come out. She cut the corner draped in a sheet, and threw Jay his shorts.

"What did she mean I need to listen to you?" he asked.

"Give her some time to cool off. I'm not at liberty to say more than that."

"Sounds like you know something I don't."

Millicent looked at the clock on the wall. "Oh shit. I forgot to cancel my date with…"

"You better not say that cop."

"He's nice. He doesn't deserve to get stood up."

"Fuck him. I got you."

"But for how long? The way you stuttered when Jen asked if you loved me says I need to tread carefully with you."

"I don't throw that word around, Mills. But I do feel something for you. And I don't want you to leave. I want you to move out of those married folk's house, and move in with me and my boy. They need privacy right now, and I don't want you to be alone. Everything is out in the open now. Let me make you feel safe. Let me take care of you."

"I can take care of myself."

"But you don't have to. Don't act like you don't know me. You know how I roll."

"That's just it. I don't know you. What's your favorite food?"

"Steak. What's yours?"

"Anything Italian. Who is your favorite rapper?"

"Snoop and Jeezy." Jay nodded his head.

"Jeezy? Really?"

"What's wrong with Jeezy?"

"Nothing's wrong with him...I mean, I like to turn on trap music in my cute clothes riding to work sometimes, but he hasn't been out long enough to be someone's favorite rapper."

"Who is yours?"

"I love J. Cole, Andre 3000, and Kendrick Lamar."

"What could your boughetto ass possibly know about Kendrick Lamar?"

"I know 'We Gon' Be Alright.'" Millicent sang in tune.

"Look at you." Jay curved the side of his lips. "Mills has a cool side."

"Don't seem so shocked."

"I took you for a Swiftee."

Millicent choked on a laugh. "The fact you know what that is, is unbelievable."

"Why? Because I look like I don't listen to Taylor Swift?"

"Name one song by her."

"This one seems appropriate after what just happened." Jay paused, staring into her eyes. "'W-e–e-Are-Never-Ever-Ever.'"

"Okay stop. I believe you." Millicent held up her hands, and the sheet covering her naked body fell to the floor.

"See we have more in common than you thought." Jay snatched the sheet. "And right now I want to get back to our unfinished business."

"What about my date?"

"Like I said earlier. Fuck the police."

Chapter 11

Which One of Us Is The Fool
Landon

Ten minutes early this time, Walt arrived at The Jeffries' home. A sudden shower formed above him, and he frowned at the sky before taking cover under the porch. He rang the doorbell, shaking off beads of water before they absorbed into his shirt.

Landon opened the door dressed in a tracksuit and sunglasses. She gasped at the flash of lightning striking behind him. A thunderous roar shook the house, and rattled the light fixture above Walt's head.

"Please come in. I can't let you stand outside in this mess." She waved him inside. "I had no idea it was supposed to rain today."

"Neither did I. Did I catch you on your way out?" He alluded to her sunglasses.

"The rain has changed those plans. I was going to go for a run and clear my head."

"Bad day?"

"I'm afraid to say I'm not alone in that department. Millicent isn't here."

"I am a little early."

"What time were your plans?"

Walt raised a brow. "You said were— as if— you don't plan on her showing up?"

Landon scowled.

Walt raised both brows. "Did something happen?"

"A lot happened."

Landon's body language and the shakiness in her voice forced Walt to switch into work mode. "I'm not in uniform, but I'm still an officer of the law. May I ask, is everything okay?" He asked, quickly getting over the news he was being stood up.

"Everything's fine. Why do you ask?"

"Your husband hasn't come to say hello. I thought we got along pretty okay last night. Millicent isn't here for our date, yet here you are telling me I've been stood up behind a pair of sunglasses on a rainy day, inside your house no less."

"I guess it's safe to say you don't know how to clock out, do you?"

"I'd feel a lot better if I could make sure you aren't hiding something behind those shades. Please?"

Landon huffed. "I'm not hiding anything. I just had a little crying spell, and my eyes are puffy."

"Still, if you don't mind." Walt insisted.

Landon lowered her lenses. "See. Puffy. I told you I'm fine." She chuckled.

"You're laughing. That's a good sign."

"I can't believe you thought I was a battered woman. Todd would never."

"He didn't give me that impression, but you never know what goes on behind closed doors. Sorry for prying. The job seems to never leave me, and I had to be sure," he said, opening the door.

"I appreciate it. It's still coming down pretty hard out there."

"Yeah, I don't think you're going to get that run in today." He gazed at Landon staring at the rain pouring onto the porch. "I'm going to make my way back to my side before the roads get flooded. Here's my card. Use it if you need anything."

"Thank you, but I don't need it. Trust me. These bags won't be under my eyes for much longer."

Walt's face twitched from her choice of words. He stepped on the porch and turned around. "Landon, if you don't mind my asking, am I wrong to think there might be something going on between Millicent and that Jay character?"

Landon snickered. "Jay character. You summed him up in one word," she replied, and turned silent.

Walt waited for her to confirm. "Well, it was nice seeing you again. You take care of yourself."

Landon closed the door and called Millicent one more time. She watched Walt strut his broad shoulders and muscular chest down the pavement through the blinds. The prompt beeped to leave a message on Millicent's voicemail, and she said, "I'm watching your shot at happiness walk away while you lay it low and wide for Jay of all people. I hope you know what you're doing."

Chapter 12

Insult to Injury

Landon

The Jeffries had become strangers in their house. The once model of what a husband should be was now cold to his better half, and she, disengaging and curt. With no resolve of the matter with the child, and Landon insistent he was not welcome in the home, the brick wall they hit stacked layers between them a bulldozer couldn't knock down.

Todd's first attempt to reconcile came weeks later, reminding her of his mother's birthday party. Landon knew it was his way of trying to find a way back into her world. She agreed to tag along, disheartened by the continued struggling conversation between them in the car. Her heart ached at every beat of silence. Her body shivered of fear. They were in uncharted waters, with no sign of rescue.

The pain in her chest grew stronger when she noticed Ephram playing outside with the other children. She sighed at Todd's lack of communication. "I should have known and should have stayed home," she said to herself.

"What's that?"

"Nothing." She mumbled below her breath. "God be with me today."

Mother Jeffries was aware of Landon's decision to postpone having a child. She pushed for her to change her mind when Todd shared the news of a spontaneous miscarriage Landon suffered while they were engaged, so it was no shock of her passive aggressive digs, and gloating about Ephram in front of the entire family.

The insurmountable sneaky looks, smirks, and pity taps on Landon's shoulder from the family were endured with grace, and a poker face, while she screamed on the inside.

"Isn't he the cutest little thing?" said Mother Jeffries.

Her sister chimed in. "He looks just like Todd and PJ when they were boys." She turned to Landon. "Wonder what y'alls baby would look like?"

Mother Jeffries turned up her nose. "We'll never know. She has a career."

"We sure won't," Landon snapped back, and made her exit.

She found herself a spot on the front porch as she waited for a cab. The smell of wood burning in the backyard comforted her as her emotions ran high, thinking of the baby she lost. She wondered if it were a boy would it have looked like him, and the pain in her chest churned, reflecting on the wound that never healed.

The more she held back her tears, the wider the pain spread. Reality sunk in she was no longer a part of Todd's family. Their marriage was over, and love wasn't enough to save them. A smile crept on her face when she least expected it. She'd arrived at the inevitable moment she feared for months. To begin a new chapter of her life and walk away gracefully, giving Todd what he desperately wanted. To be a father.

PJ appeared out of nowhere, standing in front of Landon,

reeking of beer, weed, and smoke from the fire out back. She gasped and jumped when he called her name.

"Landon, whatchu doing out here by yourself?"

"Getting some fresh air. Where did you come from?"

PJ pointed to the side of the house. "You were gone just now. What's on my favorite sister-in-law's mind?"

"You got another one I don't know about?" Landon smiled.

PJ laughed. "Yeah, I do. You know Nardo, my sister's husband. That's the biggest bitch I know."

They both cackled.

"I know you're out here 'cause them hens is clucking inside, ain't they?"

Landon rolled her eyes.

"Todd told me what's going on. I hate y'all having problems. My brother has always been crazy about you. To see you two fizzle out over something like this. Be tough, Sis. Don't let nobody come in and fuck up what the two of y'all got."

"I can't compete with a man and his seed."

"I told my brother he should have put his foot up that boy's ass and handled it. That was some fucked up shit to say. I don't know, Sis. I'm witchu on this one. I've been to jail more times than I care to think of, and it ain't no place for the likes of you. I wouldn't want to be around the little joker either if he said some shit like that to me either."

"PJ, you are the only person who agrees with me. Thank you for helping me realize I am not crazy."

"You ain't crazy. These kids on some next shit these days. It's a little bad ass down the street that talks so much shit to me when I walk to the corner store. I ride Little Man's bike past his house to make the insults go by faster."

Landon held her side laughing. "What does he say to you?"

"One time he followed me and called me a mama's boy. Said I was still teetin,' and my teeth was gonna rotten from suckin' old ass sour milk. Last week, I thought I was in the clear. His little ass shoulda been in school, but he was home playing hooky. That little fucker lifted up the window and shouted, "Fuck you, punk ass PJ, with your dirty bitch ass!"

"No he didn't." Landon cackled.

"I ain't lying. I threw a rock at his window. I'm a bust his little ass one day."

Landon held her chest as the pain subsided but grew tight from the heavy laughter PJ blessed her with.

"I needed that laugh. But don't go back to jail beating up somebody's child."

"That's where you're wrong. That ain't a child. That's a demon hiding inside a kid's body. Fuck them kids."

The taxi drove up, and Landon bounced from the porch. "Do me a favor and tell your brother I'm gone."

"No, Sis. Don't just up and leave. You know how family is."

"I do. But I don't think I'm a part of this one anymore." Landon blew PJ a kiss. "See you 'round, maybe."

In the back of the cab, Landon's tears dropped like water from a faucet. The faces of all of her friends flashed in her head to call for comfort, but the only one she wanted to hear from was Jen.

With murmured speech and endless sniffles, she managed to greet Jen coherently. "Can you talk?"

"Always for you. What's going on? Millicent sleeping with your man too?" Jen joked.

Landon screamed out a laugh, and her cry paused. "How did you say that calm and carefree?"

"Chile, I'm over it. I hope your friend is happy with her community peen. Now were you crying, or was I hearing things?"

"I was, but thanks to you I'm crying and laughing. I'm glad I called you."

"Talk to me."

"Todd and I are over."

"Don't say that."

"We are."

"You wouldn't be crying if you didn't still love him."

"I will always love him, but I can't live like this. Neither of us are happy, and the only person who agrees with me is PJ."

"Now Landon, I'm on your side too. But I wouldn't go around bragging that PJ is your support system with his crazy ass." Jen chuckled.

"PJ is cool. But you wanna know something eerie?"

"Besides the fact you are listening to PJ, please."

"The little boy looks more like him than he does Todd."

Jen scoffed. "That happens in families though."

"But remember when this first came to light the guys said the mother got around?"

"I see where you're going, but Landon, he took a test. It's his son. I don't think you're ever going to make peace with that."

"You're right. I don't know why I'm backtracking. I've already made up my mind. I am going to file. I feel like Todd wants to, but he's doing that man thing where they push the woman to take action so the blame doesn't reside with him."

"I know exactly what you mean. Men do stupid shit like that all the time. Fucking cowards." Jen clicked her teeth. "You should come down here before making any moves. Come help me with my makeup bar and step away for a while."

"If I won't be imposing I'd love to get away for a few days."

"Call me with your flight details. Can't wait to see you."

The invitation to visit Jen didn't rust. Landon arrived home and booked the next flight down to Miami in the morning. Todd stumbled in the house as she packed for her trip.

"So that's it? You just leave and don't say shit to me?" Todd griped.

"I'm sure I wasn't missed."

Todd's speech slurred. "Why are you packing bags at this hour? You ain't going nowhere, Landon. You my wife. You carry my last name."

"I know I do. I'm going to spend a few days with Jen."

"You didn't discuss that with me." He snatched a blouse from her suitcase.

"We haven't discussed anything in weeks. Todd, you are out of your mind right now. The first conversation between us should not be when you're like this."

He threw her blouse on the floor. "You got something to say to me, then say it."

"Did you drive home like this?"

"Why you care? You left and didn't say shit to me. Don't you never pass messages to me through my brother again. You hear me?"

Landon sighed, holding in her laugh at how ridiculous he sounded. She picked up her blouse and placed it back in her luggage. Todd threw it back to the floor.

"Stop packing this fucking bag. You not going to see no Jen and get hooked up with one of Pretty Ricky's boy toys."

Landon laughed in his face.

"Don't laugh at me. I ain't say shit funny." He grabbed her and held her close. "I miss you, baby. Why you wanna leave me?"

"I'm not leaving you. I'm just going to see my friend for a few days."

"No." Todd sniffed her neck. "You always smell so good. Look what you did." He placed her hand on his manhood.

"I'm not fucking you like this. Get over yourself."

"You know you want to." Todd snickered.

Landon huffed. "I have something to ask you."

"Go ahead. Ask me anything baby."

"Is there a chance Ephram is PJ's son, and not yours?"

Todd pushed Landon away and looked at her in a way she'd never seen before. His red eyes, filled with hatred and disdain for her narrowed, and his voice raised so loudly, she was sure the neighbors heard their quarrel.

"I took a fucking test, Landon! It's just a child. They lie, They tell stories. They do bullshit. Give it a rest!"

Landon shuddered. "You know what, you're right. I am giving it a rest."

"What does that mean?"

Landon threw more clothing in her suitcase and stuffed her duffel bag until it overflowed and wouldn't zip.

"You've made a big deal about nothing. All you had to do was let it go. Why'd you do this to us baby? Huh?"

"Todd, I have wrestled with this for far too long. I can't anymore. You have been mad at me for how I reacted, and that isn't fair. We'll never agree on this, and I've made my peace with it. My flight leaves in the morning. I'll be back in a few days. We can talk about a separation when I get back, and when you're sober."

"I'm not leaving. You are the one talking about walking away."

Landon faced Todd and gazed into his eyes for the first time in weeks, searching for the version of him she once knew. The version she fell in love with. The husband that made her feel nothing came before her. He wasn't there.

"Todd, if Ephram had fallen, and I was the one to find him, I wonder would I somehow be blamed for that too."

"Landon, just let it go."

"And there's my answer!" Tears poured from her eyes. "No matter how that day played out, it's clear we are no longer what we once were. You are attached to another woman, and there isn't anything to change that. When I get back I'm filing for divorce, and I want to get through this as amicably as possible."

Landon stormed out of their bedroom and Todd ran after her. Down the stairs he stumbled, holding onto the railing and yelling in a drunken stupor. "We're not getting a divorce! What's gotten into you?! How you gon' leave me, girl? You know you love me. I'll unpack all those fuckin' bags! You hear me!"

"Don't follow me. Go sleep that shit off at Jay's house or something."

"I'm not leaving this house! You gonna have to burn this motherfucker down with me in it. I ain't leaving my house and you ain't leaving it either!"

Todd pressed on Landon's heels from room to room, cornering her in the kitchen. "Come here girl," he said in the low, slick tone that used to entice her. "You don't want me no more, baby?" He kissed her lips. Landon squirmed in his arms and blew a raspberry from her mouth. "Remember what we did on the counter a while back?"

"Todd, go to sleep! Please."

"I don't want to go to sleep. I wanna make love to my wife. You see what you do to me." He pressed his dick against her folds. "You don't wanna leave me. Do you? Tell me you were just bullshittin'."

Buzzing from his phone vibrated between them. Todd grinned on the side of his mouth and kissed Landon again. "I saw that look in your eye. That got you excited. You been handling business without me these past weeks." He cracked himself up and nibbled on her ear. "Where you keep your toys? Show me what you've been doing."

Landon maneuvered from his clutch. "Just answer your phone."

Todd's face turned squeamish when he answered, "Yeah."

Derailed

"Thank you for letting E come today. He said he had a good time," Ephram's mother said faintly through the phone.

Landon shook her head and slapped her thigh.

Todd studied the aggravation in her face and stuttered. "Okay."

"He also mentioned your mother said you and your wife are having problems. If that's true, we can go on and give this a shot of being a family. E would love that."

"Nah, that's not true. And that's not happening. Is there a reason you're calling?"

"I just told you. People get together for the sake of their children all the time. You think about that."

He ended the call and held his head down. "I'll talk to my mother."

"No need. This isn't the marriage I signed up for."

Chapter 13

I've Been Drinking & I've Been Thinking

Jen

Buried below Todd's arm, Landon slid to the side of the bed and escaped the hungover madness before it began. She arrived in Miami an emotional wreck, crying at the sight of Jen waiting for her at baggage claim.

"Stop crying. You're going to make me cry, and I'm trying to advertise my business." Jen teased.

"Take me to see it."

Tears rolled down Landon's cheek as she admired the light in Jen's face walking her through the make-up bar.

"You did it. You left behind all that toxic shit, and look at you. You're thriving. It's like you have a whole new life. You've given me hope."

"So your decision is final?" Jen squeezed her shoulder.

"I told him last night."

"So it's a heavy drinking kind of night, huh?"

"Let's start now."

Jules kept the drinks flowing while Landon and Jen hung outside at the pool.

"Are you sure you don't want me to call some friends over? Have a little party to get your mind off things?" he asked.

"I'm positive. This view and my friend is all I need."

"Let me know if you change your mind. Babe, I'm going to go make that run. Call me if you need anything."

"I'll be back, Landon. Let me walk him out."

Before the sun set, Landon was drawn into the waves roaring under the near dusk sky. She closed her eyes, placed her feet in the azure water and held her arms out wide. The breeze calmed the raging, confused spirit she brought with her to Miami, and the water cleansed her clouded mind. When she opened her eyes, she witnessed the sun slide below the blue horizon, and dropped a tear into the Atlantic.

"You alright?" Jen stood at her side.

"I think so." Landon pointed towards the sunset. " That was us. Falling off into the unknown."

"And like tomorrow morning, we'll rise again." Jen held her hand.

"I haven't listened to his messages. I feel free not hearing his voice. That's a good thing, right?"

"None of this is good, but it's a start to moving on. Don't let your thoughts beat you up. Hear me?"

"I'll try not to."

"Mine did for weeks. Most of all Milli Vanilli's fake ass. I think she hurt me more than Jay. I can't make sense of it." Jen kicked the water.

"Because you expected something like that from him."

"Right. Jay sticking and moving doesn't surprise me. But with her? Who would have ever thought?"

"Millicent's date. That's who." Landon laughed. "Poor guy drove all the way back to the city in the pouring rain the next day, and Millicent left him hanging. His instincts are sharp, that one.

He asked if something was going on between them, and I had to cover for her when I was at my absolute worst."

"That guy was hot as fuck."

"Smoking!" Landon and Jen tossed water on each other.

"I'm glad Millicent fumbled that. As much as I am mad about what she's done, I still win."

"What do you mean?"

"I have Jules, and she has Jay." Jen spun around in the water dancing and screaming. "But now I have to rethink Jay having custody of Max. I don't want my baby calling Millicent 'Mommy.' I'd...You know."

Landon was familiar with that tone. Chills ran down her spine while her imagination ran wild on how Jen would have finished that sentence. She ended the silence with a confession.

"I'm going to be honest. Our friendship hasn't been the same lately either. I find myself questioning if she would have done the same thing to me."

"And you're wise to ask that question. I found myself thinking about some of the questionable things she's done and said over the years. Do you remember on our girls' trip when she said you were living vicariously through me in regards to an old flame?"

"Yes! I was pissed she brought that up! She was talking about my old crush, Reynaldo, back in Flint. The star of the baseball team who broke up with me and had everybody calling me DT."

"What is that?"

"A dick teaser." Landon blushed. "I deserved that nickname. I was too afraid of the dick back then, and I led on a lot of guys but never put out. I was a good girl." Landon laughed. "Until one night, I came real close to doing it with ole Rey Rey. We kissed and kissed and kissed until there was nothing left to kiss, so naturally he did what any horny teenage boy would do. He whipped his shit out and blinded my ass. I hadn't seen a lot of penises in real time, but I know the one I had in my hands would have destroyed my virgin ass. It was priceless."

Jen fell to her knees in the water laughing. "Priceless? Was it gold or something?"

"It should have been. It looked like one of those mushrooms you see growing out in a country field standing tall above the other shrooms that weren't so blessed. Wide, long, and pretty. Like I said, priceless."

"I may have to call Jules back for a quickie hearing you talk like this."

"I'm getting flustered myself just thinking about it. Anyway, Millicent knows that I will carry that moment with me forever. Before I met Todd, I confessed to her that I wanted to go back home and find him, have my way with him to kill the curiosity of what it felt like to be with such a man."

"Well, you might become a free woman soon. There's time to fulfill that dream, and if it's anything like me and Jules finding each other again, it's going to be so explosive I might feel it down here." Jen and Landon chuckled. "All this talk about pretty pipes has me riled up. Wear your earplugs tonight."

As Landon listened to her hosts moan, and the bed knock against the wall, her legs squeezed tightly around her hand. Her fingers rotated above her panties as eroticized thoughts owned her body. She was weeks without pleasure, thinking of the hard dick she left begging to please her at home. Her mind wandered, imagining Todd's lips against her nipples as Jules groaned in the other room loud enough to make her want to offer herself to whichever friend he said he could invite over.

Their echoes of pleasure invaded her mind, remembering the make-up fuck sessions she and Todd had over the years. How he made her scream with passion and climb the walls with spontaneous bouts of love making at any given time of the day. The more Jen shrieked of ecstasy, the raunchier her thoughts traveled, back to the high school lover she regretted passing over.

She replayed the night she nearly lost her virginity in her head. Her white shorts pulled to the side, her cotton bikinis shredded in the seat of her folds, and Reynaldo sucking all the juice from her cup. She grinded his face from the top of the slide on the playground where the shade from the trees blocked out the street light. His nose stimulated her clit, his hungry eyes looked up at her, begging her to agree to let him put in the tip.

"I'll let you do the finger," she said.

Reynaldo grinned at her permission, spread her soaked lips apart with his fingers, and hunched her with his dick about to rip through his briefs.

"I can tell you want to," he whispered.

"I do, but I'm scared."

"Don't be. I know what I'm doing."

"I don't want to get pregnant my first time."

"You won't."

"And I don't want to get called a heaux."

"Nobody's going to know."

He relieved his cock from the pressure overflowing in his shorts and rubbed it against her thigh. Landon jumped, "What's that?" she asked.

"That's how excited I am to be with you right now." Reynaldo lied.

Landon stroked his penis, disgusted by the fluid leaking out, and terrified at the girth between her palm.

"I'm still not ready. What if I give you a hand job?"

"Landon, I can't keep doing this with you." Reynaldo's soft tone turned harsh.

"I'm sorry. I'm just not ready."

"I was damn near in. Come on. Don't leave me like this." Reynaldo's foot slipped from the bottom step.

Landon covered her exposed nature and giggled. "See that's a sign. I can't let my first time be on a dirty park slide. Walk me home."

"Nah. You walk yourself."

Landon woke from the dream and opened her eyes. The grunts stopped next door, so did her recollection of the past. She reached for the light, unsatisfied and beaten as her phone lit with a text from Todd. *'Come home.'*

Jen found Landon sitting out on the deck at day break, stretched out beneath a blanket with a bottle of wine resting on the end table.

"Morning," said Landon, tipping her glass to Jen's empty hand.

"Are we skipping the mimosas and diving straight in today?"

"If I can stomach it. This is my second bottle. I'll pay you for them."

"Don't be silly." Jen placed the empty bottles in the blue bin. "Something set you off?"

"Todd. He messaged me last night. Two words. *'Come home'*."

"So you saw the flowers?"

"What flowers?"

"Jules left them on the table. I thought they were for me, but the card said those exact same words. *'Come home.'*"

Landon scoffed. "I would prefer we didn't spend my last night here talking about him."

"Done. What do you want to do?"

"Honestly. Sleep."

"That's depression talking."

"And I welcome it. If you and Jules don't mind, I'd like to lie around all day and do absolutely nothing."

Jen wiped the tear strolling down her cheek. "You got it. Give me a holler if you need me."

"Thanks. I knew I came to the right place."

The sun circled the house while Landon drank and napped. Jen snuck in her room and left cheese, crackers, and mini sandwiches by her bed for when she woke, switching out her tray with fresh fruit and toasted bagels when she emerged the next morning. Landon hauled her luggage down the steps.

"Jen, you are a lifesaver. I don't know where I would be without you. Thank you for taking care of me."

"I love you like a sister."

"You are my sister. Remember that."

Chapter 14

Home Not So Sweet Home

Todd

Landon returned and dropped the bomb Todd feared. He sat on the edge of the bed with the world shut off, processing the words *trial separation* in his head.

His eyes were glued to the floor as Landon pranced in and out of the bedroom, glancing at him from the corner of her eyes, waiting for him to make a move or a sound. His lack of response made her break a sweat, and the confidence she lied to herself about, slowly crumbled.

"That's the second time you've said you don't want to be in this marriage," Todd mumbled. "What's going on? You hate me now or something?"

"I don't hate you. But you know as well as I do this isn't working."

"But you think living separate lives will work? Splitting up is not how you fix problems."

"Some problems can't be fixed. This is that problem."

"You are overreacting about this like a motherfucker." The muscles in Todd's arms flexed.

"Staying together when joy has been stripped from a union is not an option for me."

"So fuck my options is what you're saying?"

"Todd, answer this. The next time I have a problem with your son, what are you going to do? Be mad at me again, punish me for having my own feelings, force me to be present when I'm uncomfortable?"

"It's a major change that's going to take some time getting used to."

"I don't want to get used to it. I'm done."

"Done? Are we separating, or going straight for a divorce?"

Landon refused to look at Todd, or give him an answer.

Todd exhaled. "If it's a divorce you want, I'll give it to you. I'm done pleading my case."

He sped off into the night, drowning his sorrows at the bar, and venting to anyone who would listen. The bartender sent word to Jay he was needed. He arrived and shared a few shots with Todd, listening to his drunken stupor and make believe scenarios. When his speech slurred, Jay cut him off and delivered him home to the woman he spent all night ranting about.

"You did a number on my boy," he said.

"You did a number on my girl." Landon sassed.

"Yeah, yeah. Take it easy on him. And cut out all that separation talk, L. You know damn well ain't nobody gonna love you like my people. I never pegged you for the selfish type. Work this shit out. You hear me?"

"Thanks for watching out for him tonight." Landon shut her door.

She covered her better half with a blanket in the guest room downstairs. Todd grabbed her hand. "Look at my pretty wife." Landon ignored him, slid her hand away, and eased to the door. She shut off the light as her husband continued to mumble. "Don't leave me baby. I love you girl. Don't leave me baby."

Derailed

His stupefied speech troubled Landon throughout the hours of the night. Guilt and fear of ending her marriage shot pains to her heart. She worried how he would take care of himself when he was on his own, and how she would manage the cold winter nights without him. With a clouded mind she tortured herself with what ifs and regret until she found herself laid next to him.

Todd inched behind her, kissed the back of her shoulder, and placed his arm around her waist. "I love you too. Don't give up on us," he said, mid-snore in his sleep.

Landon lied with him until the sun crept through the thin sheers on the window. Todd reached for her with one hand, and grabbed his morning wood with the other, expecting to grind his way back into his wife's good graces.

"Landon!" He sat up on the bed.

She popped her head inside the room. "Coffee is on the stove. It should help with that hangover."

"I'd prefer some of your coffee." Todd patted the sheets.

Landon blushed.

"Did I imagine you in my arms last night?" he asked, rubbing the crust from his eyes.

"No. I kept you company."

"You know next to me is where you'll always belong."

"Then keep it warm for me in ten years. I'm running late. Let's put a pin in this until tonight."

Work didn't distract Landon's mind from wrestling with her heart for a win. She enjoyed sleeping next to Todd, being in that familiar space of protection and love. In a haste, she prepared to escape the confines of being reeled in by her husband's charm and devilish good looks. He arrived home with flowers, candy, and passes for a matinee to the first movie they saw, blindsided with a note waiting for him under a magnet on the fridge.

I'll be working remotely for the rest of the week. Headed to my parents for a few days. We'll talk when I get back.

Chapter 15

She Went to Flint
Landon

Mother Davis knew the surprise visit from her eldest daughter came with the need of wisdom and approval. She welcomed the younger version of herself with loving arms and suspicion, happy to know she was still needed in her headstrong daughter's life.

Landon crossed over the Davis Family doormat, rushed by memories of her childhood. The fights between her and her younger sister Launa, standing on the stool to help her mother cook dinner, and the day she left for college, oblivious she would never live there anymore. The scent of blackberry cobbler and coffee stained in the walls brought the taste to the tip of her tongue. The pictures of her and Launa at prom hanging in the living room brought a smile to her face as she passed the hallway where the many talent show awards dressed the shelves near the piano.

Landon stopped and stared at the life size painting of her grandmother gracing the top of the staircase. It held her attention for so long, everything faded into the background.

"What brings you home?"

Landon gasped. "I didn't hear you walk up. Nice to see you too."

"That's no way to welcome your sister, is it, Launa?" Mother Davis chastised.

"I didn't mean anything by it, but seriously, when does Landon ever come home and it's not a holiday? Must be trouble in paradise."

"Why are you like this?" asked Landon. "Don't answer that. I know it's because you've been stuck here your entire life."

"And look who came back." Launa smirked.

"Girls."

"Sorry, Mama. I won't be staying long. This one has me already cutting my visit shorter than I planned."

"I hear fussing," Mr. Davis interrupted.

"Daddy!" Landon pushed Launa out of the way.

"Look at you. It's like looking at your mother all those years ago." Papa Davis wrapped his frail arms around Landon.

"Yay. Daddy's favorite daughter remembered where he lives," Launa mumbled.

"Chile, be happy we're all together again, and hush up with all that griping and carrying on. I thought you had to go to work?" Mother Davis added.

"On my way like a good soldier." Launa laughed at her sarcasm alone. "Tough crowd. Don't forget Tim's bus will be here at 3:15."

"I don't need reminding." Mother Davis fanned her off.

Landon shook her head at her sister talking under her breath, stomping down the stairs. Mother Davis sighed and rubbed the sides of her face with her palms.

"Just once I wish my prayer came true and you girls got along."

"We do get along. Once she gets all of that hostility out, we'll be fine."

Derailed

"I hope so. I don't want you to cut your stay short. But to what do we owe the pleasure?" Mother Davis asked. "Is she right about trouble in paradise? I don't see your better half with you."

"I did come home to share some news in person, and get your advice on a certain matter."

"Well, let's go into the kitchen. This sounds like it calls for comfort food."

Mother Davis pulled out pots, pans, leftover dinner, and filled a bowl with butter and flour. As she rolled fresh biscuits, Landon and her dad sat at the breakfast table where her nephew, Tim, drew pencil and crayon markings into the wood.

"It's like looking into a time machine, baby girl."

"I wish to age as beautifully as Mama."

Landon's natural coiled hair was exactly like her mother's. She shared her light brown eyes, symmetrical face, and full lips, but took after father with a light brown complexion. The only feature she and Launa shared. Launa, on the other hand, was her father's child. A spitting image of him with coarser and fuller hair, with nothing of Laura Lee except for her petite shape and small feet.

As the chicken boiled and the biscuits entered the oven, Mother Davis probed Landon to find out what was going on.

"How is my son-in-law?"

"Pretty upset with me. I came home because I wanted to tell you in person that I've decided to file for a divorce. I know this is not what marriage is about, and I wish I could have stuck it out like you two, but we have a situation that is not going to go away anytime soon, and I am unhappy."

"Well, I was hoping for the good news of a possible grandchild." Father Davis sighed.

"But Todd is a good boy." Mother Davis dropped her hand from her hip. "I don't understand. Did he put hands on you? Cheat on you?"

"No, and not that I know of."

"Well, if he didn't cheat on you or beat on you, it must be you."

"I guess I am to blame. I said for better or for worse, but the worse involves a child he fathered before we met, and the little boy has been causing us to have problems."

"How old is the boy?"

"Eight."

"I'm not happy about hearing the word divorce. What kind of problems is the boy causing?"

"He threatened to put me in jail for pushing him down the stairs."

Mother Davis held her chest. "What kind of child is this? And what did Todd say?"

Landon's voice choked. "In a nutshell, I need to get over it."

Father Davis scoffed, "Baby girl, I love Todd. And I trusted him with your hand. But if he isn't making you feel like the diamond you are, I'll support you leaving. I know you love him, so it must be pretty bad in your house if you want to end your marriage with him."

Her mother smacked her father's arm. "Don't be so hasty. Aren't you afraid of being alone, Landon? Your sister says there aren't any good men out there, and judging from what she's brought home, she is telling the truth. They don't make'em like they used to. And Todd is a good one. Careful you haven't already driven him into the arms of another woman while yours end up empty."

"I can survive on my own, Mama."

"I'm not talking about survival. I'm talking about loneliness." Mother Davis kissed her teeth. "It's okay to weather some storms."

Father Davis interrupted, "But Laura Lee, some storms come around and wipe shit out, leaving people to start from scratch. If you need a new start, your Daddy has your back."

Mother Davis threw her hands up. "I guess my advice ain't worth a damn."

Landon kissed her mother. "Of course it is. Just have my back when Launa throws this in my face."

"Don't pay your sister no mind. She has no room to talk."

"What you know, Mama?"

Mother Davis tightened her lips and removed the biscuits from the oven humming a church hymn to stop from spreading family gossip Landon knew the sound of her mother's hymn meant to move on. She admired the handmade crafts her nephew created that lined the kitchen walls while her dad updated her on his plans for retirement, and schooling her about putting her money into separate bank accounts before the legal proceedings.

"You know who else is divorced? The Felix boy from down the street. Wife took him to the cleaners. He had to move home."

"I'm not worried about that, Daddy."

"You know who ain't never got married? Reynaldo. Saw him at the football game last Friday night."

Landon's interest grew in her father's stories after hearing Reynaldo's name. His admiration for the former baseball star increased her curiosity of how he turned out after so many years. She chuckled internally, recalling her recent conversation about him with Jen.

"How is Reynaldo? I haven't heard that name in years."

Mother Davis raised a brow.

Papa Davis smiled. "He's doing good. Took an assistant coaching job at your alma mater."

"Really? Good for him."

"You know, I always thought you would end up with him. Thought I was going to be flying off to games, sitting in a sky box somewhere watching him play."

"I don't know why you thought that, Daddy. We were kids. Nothing serious."

"You were stuck on those old rich boys from across the bridge. Only my daughter would give the baseball star the pink slip to chase pretty boys."

"It was all for the best. You dodged a bullet." Mother Davis winked at her.

Landon gave her mother the side eye before excusing herself to unpack her car. She settled in her old room and napped before her nephew made it home from school, demanding the attention of everyone in the house. His footsteps stomped up and down the hallway, waking Landon. She listened to him make noise throughout the house, putting a stop to it with a kiss to his forehead. "You've gotten so big." She stole sugar from his cheek. Tim blushed and sat down, studying the aunt he hadn't seen in months.

Landon recognized the way she interacted with her nephew was how she wished she interacted with Ephram. Quickly she recognized the difference, and her decision became clearer than it had before. She knew she was making the right choice to set Todd free to be a father, and begin her journey to finding the happiness she'd lost.

Launa strolled in after dinner. Landon sat on the screened porch in the dark, snickering at her loose walk coming down the sidewalk.

"You party through the week, I see." Landon dug at her.

"I thought you would have been halfway back to your bougie world by now. Tell me, how has the world come crashing down on your head?" Launa laughed.

"Silly of me to wait out here for you with hopes we could talk like sisters for once. What was I thinking? I must be crazy for trying."

"You called me a heaux the last time you wanted to have a sisterly chat. You remember that?"

"Yeah, I remember." Landon snickered. "I wouldn't have called you that if you weren't so nasty to me."

"Doesn't sound like an apology."

"You know what, never mind." Landon opened the door to go inside.

"That's right." Launa clapped her hands. "Run off like always. Run back to your degree and your big house and your stuck up husband thinking y'all are better than everybody else."

"I don't walk around thinking I'm better than anyone, and Todd is far from stuck up. You're just mad I left you behind."

"Don't act like you are my savior, L boogie. What you gonna do? You gon' rescue me? You gon' take me under your wing and make me dress like you and act like you? No thanks."

"Just tell me what I did that caused you to hate me so much."

"Ain't nobody got time to be hatin' you. You don't make my world go round."

Landon stormed into the house. Launa stayed behind on the porch and sat where her sister had. "It's good to have you home, Sis." She raised her glass punch bottle and took a swig.

The next morning, Tim asked his aunt to drive him to school. "My friends said you have the coolest car," he said. Launa gritted her teeth at his request. Landon happily did what her nephew asked of her, getting a brief taste of what life would be like as a mom. For two days she got up early every morning, rushed to get two people out of the house, helped her mom take care of the home, prepared meals, and caught up with her work. And after those two days, she understood why her sister was so bitter and angry.

Neither sister apologized with words. They carried on as if jabs hadn't been exchanged, and softened up to each other during the rest of Landon's visit, finally making progress on improving their bond. Hearing her girls laugh and carry on a conversation without discord was music to Laura Lee's ears.

"Maybe now your daddy will take you three to the game with him. He's been wanting to ask you, but with the way you two have been acting, he's been dancing around it."

Landon and Launa looked at each other and laughed.

"You want to tell him?" Launa asked.

"You do it. I'll go get changed." Landon dashed to her old room.

The field was packed with old classmates and their children, local college scouts, and former frenemies of The Davis Girls, the one thing that would always unite them. They put on airs and gossiped like the best of friends, whispering in each other's ear about the people they came across in the stands.

Landon had forgotten how good the hot dogs were at the ball field stand, and after devouring the one her dad bought, she offered to pay for the second round of dogs, peanuts, and Coke. She stood in the long line cheering on the home team as they scored, looking back at her sister laughing at how ridiculous she looked making all that noise by herself.

The line cleared ahead in front of her, and she stepped ahead to order. "I thought I would never lay eyes on you again." Reynaldo Williams' low voice rumbled in her ear.

Landon turned around to big white teeth and wet lips. "Hey, you. I thought the same thing."

"I'm glad I was wrong." He licked his lips.

"Un-huh."

"Did your old man tell you I ran into him the other day?"

"I can't say that he has." Landon lied with a sly smile on her lips. "How are you?"

"Doing good. Working as a coach at the school. I can see for myself how you're doing. Still fine as hell after all these years."

Landon blushed until her face turned red, thinking about

what she and Jen discussed. She examined his handsome face, and athletic build, noticing the only change about him was he had grown a mustache on his baby face, and gotten his ear pierced. The smell of his woodsy cologne was still the same, and when the wind blew it danced across her nose, bringing back the memory of the night they shared in the park.

"You don't look too bad yourself," she replied.

"How long has it been?"

"Six, seven years maybe." Landon shrugged.

"I mean how long has it been since that night?"

A man interrupted. "Ma'am, are you going to order?"

"Uh, yeah sure. Four hot dogs, three cokes and one bag of peanuts."

"That'll be fifteen dollars," said the clerk.

"Don't worry about it. It's on me," Reynaldo offered.

"You don't have to do that."

"I insist."

The old lovers stepped to the side as the order was being prepared. Reynaldo talked nonstop about his injury that ended his college career, and how thankful he was to be able to coach the sport he loved. The people in the line and behind the counter stared at them playing catch up, and when the food was ready, Reynaldo helped Landon take her order to the stands, making Papa Davis all smiles in the bleachers.

Chapter 16

That Old Thing
Landon

While Launa and Tim cheered on the plays, Reynaldo sat next to Papa Davis and talked his way into a dinner invitation. Landon and Launa shared a disapproving look.

"What is happening right now?" Launa asked.

"I wish I knew. Make him stop," Landon whispered.

When the conversation between Reynaldo and their father finally offered a segue, the old flame asked Landon, "Care to take a walk?"

Landon whispered to Launa. "I'll try to undo the damage daddy's done. I'm not divorced yet."

"Say what?" Launa stopped sipping from her cup.

"Yeah. You and I have a lot to catch up on. Be right back."

Reynaldo didn't beat around the bush. He asked Landon to meet him at the park where they created the memory stuck in her head. Hesitant to answer, she fumbled over words to disinvite him to dinner.

"If I say yes, will you find a reason to cancel having dinner at my parents house?"

"If you say I'll get some alone time to catch up with you properly, I'll let your pops down easy."

Landon chuckled. "Right. Then, yes, I'll see you at the playground."

Upon her return to the bleachers, she assured her sister the crisis had been averted.

"Good." Launa sighed.

"By chance, do you know why Ma said I dodged a bullet with that one?"

Launa scowled. "Why? What did he say to you down there?"

"I got him to promise not to come to dinner if I hung out with him tonight. Should I cancel? I'm curious what Ma knows about him."

"You know how old ladies gossip in church. You'd be amazed how much you think you know about a person, then the saints and sanctified blabs out your business, and you're stuck clutching your pearls in the pew. What's going on with you and Todd?"

"He has a son who has ruined our marriage. I'm filing for a divorce. End of story. You were right. Trouble in paradise."

"I didn't want to be right. Sorry about that."

"It's not your fault."

Launa held her sister's hand. "Be careful tonight. Don't think for one second you need to back pedal because you and Todd are uncertain right now. Okay?"

Whatever Laura Lee and Launa knew ate away at Landon, bugging her to pieces. It was all she could wonder about as she looked at the night sky in Reynaldo's eyes. The park was dimly lit below the moonlight, but illuminated just enough she didn't worry her old flame would try anything out in the open.

Slightly bigger than when they were teens, his five-foot-eleven frame made his chest stand robust in his t-shirt. His amber brown eyes stared into hers as his moist, kissable lips puckered at her with ill intent. Landon maneuvered her way over to the swings set. They laughed like children as Reynaldo pushed her back and forth, reciting his smooth lines from back in the day as if he were trapped in the past. The swing stopped in the air, and Reynaldo closed in on Landon from the rear. His hands wrapped around her waist, gently gliding to her thighs. She shivered from his touch, freaked out by the pounding in her chest and set of hands fondling her that didn't belong to her husband. "We weren't so lucky on the ladder last time. Maybe the swings will allow fate to finally take place." He whispered in her ear, spreading her legs apart.

Landon removed his hands and hopped off of the swing. "What's your big secret?"

"I don't know what you mean."

"I think you do."

"If you have something to ask me, just ask me."

"That's just it. I've been given a sprinkle here and there, but no one will come right out and say whatever it is you're hiding."

"Is this why you don't want me to come to dinner?"

"Sort of."

"I don't know why she didn't just tell you." He exhaled deeply. "Did your sister tell you to uninvite me?"

"She did."

Reynaldo grinned. "Your sister is jealous of you."

"I beg your pardon." Landon rolled her hips to the side.

"We kind of hooked up when you left for college."

Landon picked up a rock and threw it at his chest. The rock gently pierced his skin below his shirt.

"Ow, girl. Shit. Let me explain."

"Why the fuck did you ask to hang out with me when you've already fucked my sister?" She threw a second rock at his dick.

"Stop, girl. It wasn't like that. The day you left for school, I came by to see you. You had already left, and your sister threw herself at me."

"So it's her fault?"

"She put the moves on me."

"And that makes you innocent?"

"Look, what happened was wrong in a sense."

"In a sense? Please. Stop talking."

"I came looking for you, and things got out of hand."

Landon laughed. "God, I feel like a fool being here with you." She sucked her teeth. "Please don't show up at our house tomorrow. It's seen enough of you, don't you think?"

Landon fled the scene in a rage and made the short walk home in record time. She stormed inside and overlooked Launa watching television in the living room.

"So?" Launa asked, startling her on her way upstairs.

Landon stepped back down and glared at her sister. "You could have just told me you fucked my boyfriend. I'm sure it made you feel absolutely superior to have that one over me all of these years."

"Sounds like he's painted me as the bad guy."

"Aren't you? You came on to him knowing how I felt about him."

"That son of a bitch lied."

Laura Lee popped in from upstairs. "What is going on down here?"

"Reynaldo is what." Launa folded her arms.

"You are my sister. I would never want your sloppy seconds. And you should never want mine."

"I knew it would come to this one day." Laura Lee sighed.

Reynaldo knocked on the door, and the ladies grew quiet. The floorboards creaked above, and Papa Davis limped down the stairs.

"Why hasn't anyone gotten the door? And why did it sound like you girls were arguing? You were getting along so well earlier."

Derailed

Launa gritted through her teeth. "Daddy, don't answer that."

"What? Child, pipe down. What's gotten into you?"

Papa Davis smiled at the sight of Reynaldo standing at the door. He welcomed inside, and all of the ladies shouted. "No!" Reynaldo paused with one foot inside and the other midstep.

"What the devil is going on?" Papa Davis asked.

"Reynaldo, don't you think it's time you came clean, Son?" Laura Lee advised.

"Come clean about what?" Papa Davis frowned at Reynaldo.

"Mr. and Mrs. Davis, I would like to apologize for any confusion I may have caused."

"We don't need the apology." Laura Lee shook her head. "You owe that to our girls."

"Mama, you knew about them all this time?" Landon held her chest.

"A mother knows everything."

"Boy, I ought to knock your ass out." Papa Davis charged at Reynaldo. Laura Lee held him back. "Why am I just finding out about this?" he asked Laura Lee.

"Because you always favored Landon, and I didn't want you to hold a mistake this big against Launa, who is desperate for you to see her the way you see her sister. She's grown so much over the years. Neither of you should hold this against her." Laura Lee looked between Landon and her husband.

"Why is this coming out now?"

"Because this weasel is using your fondness of him to work his way back into the picture knowing good and well what he has done. That takes a special kind of lowdown selfishness, don't you think, Son?" Laura Lee scolded Reynaldo with her eyes.

"Ma'am, I truly am sorry. I came by tonight to apologize."

"To which one of my girls?"

Reynaldo stuttered. "Um...I um..."

"I have a question. Did it end between you two because

Mama found out, or did he throw you away after he got what he wanted?"

"I ended it." Launa confessed. She turned to Reynaldo. "You want to tell her why, or will you lie about that too?"

Reynaldo huffed. "Can I see him?"

"See who?" Papa Davis fumed.

"My son."

Landon's shoulders wilted as she looked at Launa. Laura Lee exhaled as the secret she had been carrying for years finally released her from its shackles, and Papa Davis dropped his head to the floor.

"This boy is Tim's father?" Papa Davis asked.

"He most certainly is, and Launa has been too ashamed to tell anyone. I can do math, sweetheart." Laura Lee pressed her lips tight.

"I would like to clear the air and say I offered to take care of the situation, but Launa chose to go through with it. Just like she knew I was in love with Landon, and she proposed that she and I get together."

"That's a lie!" Launa yelled.

"No, it isn't." Laura Lee intervened. "I was sitting in the living room listening that day. You were flirting with this boy, and he was so horned up he didn't care where he got it from."

Landon threw her head back at Launa.

"I'm not the only one you need to be pissed with," Launa pleaded to Landon. "There's more you don't know."

"How is that even possible?"

"I'll show myself out." Reynaldo edged for the door.

Papa Davis shut it closed. "You can leave after we discuss your responsibilities, Son."

"Landon, as bad as this looks, I do love you. I'm sorry for what happened years ago, but when you met Todd and found the happiness you deserve, I hated myself for what I'd done. And I think you should know everything has worked in your favor by not taking up with the likes of him." Launa pointed to Reynaldo. "The day I found out I was pregnant, I went to tell him, but when I got to his house, he was kissing another girl in his driveway."

"Is that why you chose to keep the baby? To spite me?"

"No, I kept my baby because I wanted him."

"None of that matters now." Papa Davis shut them up. "The boy is here now. Son, you gon' ahead and get out of here. I need to think if having the likes of you around is a good idea."

Reynaldo looked at the family ignoring his existence without a glance in his direction. He left the Davis home, and with the air cleared, Landon and Launa shared their realest conversation in years.

"What you did hurts, but not to the point I would ever disown you as my sister," Landon confessed.

"Even when I act like I hate you, I love you still." Launa reached for a hug.

"I'll always choose my sister over a mister." Landon squeezed her tightly.

"I can't breathe." Launa gasped.

"Good. That's for being stupid." She squeezed tighter. "And that's for being bitchy all of these years. Well, maybe you weren't bitchy. You were acting out of shame."

Launa fought her way out of Landon's grip. "You win. And again, I'm sorry. But there's something else you should know."

"Un uh. I don't want to know anything else that's going to gut me. Be a loving sister and bury it with you."

Chapter 17

Stronger Than Pride

Todd

The Jeffries began playing the game of who could outdo the other with the separation in tow. Todd didn't receive Landon's note well, and being the first time she went home without him spoke volumes she was serious about calling it quits on their life together. As the days went on without a phone call from her, he decided to move out of the house, and into the back room of his print shop.

The transition of living out of his beautiful home and into the mediocre living quarters of one room with a mini fridge and microwave, old television, and leather sofa were humbling and depressing. Jay's constant intrusive thoughts didn't help Todd's mental or emotional state.

"You put yourself here, man. You haven't known that kid for eight years. I wouldn't have let him come into my life, and take away everything I love. Look at you, man. No house. No good woman. And back in the streets with gold diggers and bitches playing more games than me."

"I'm not worried about bitches. This is temporary. I'll let

Landon see she and I can't be apart for too long, then we'll find our way back to each other. Everything will work itself out."

"If you say so. But if I were you, I wouldn't stay here long. I'd move my ass back in my house and live like *The War of the Roses*. I wouldn't let no muthafucka get next to L if I were you."

"I'll win her back at McCaine's anniversary party next weekend."

"And what if she doesn't miss you?"

"She will."

The night of the party, Todd surprised Landon on their doorstep with a corsage attached to a gift wrapped box with a diamond tennis bracelet inside. He complimented her as he always did. "Forever the prettiest woman at the party. If you don't mind, I would love to be your date." His puppy eyes looked up at her standing in the entrance like he was lost. And he was without her.

Landon lowered her head and smiled. "Sure. Let me grab my bag. Come in."

Confidence filled him as he stepped inside, pacing the floor and smiling to himself as the first part of his plan worked. Landon made her way back down the stairs, capturing Todd's full attention. He couldn't resist how stunning she appeared, floating in the fluorescent light like an angel without wings. Marveling at her beauty, he fought to hold his tongue in his mouth when she stepped in front of him. Todd extended his arm. "Allow me." He placed the corsage on her wrist and fastened the bracelet on the other. "Shall we?" He leaned in and stole a kiss from her cheek.

The date was a mind fuck on both of their parts. Slipping into old habits of familiarity and love as Landon had no intention of changing her mind, and Todd had no resolution regarding the scale that weighed against him– His wife on one side, his son on the other.

Their friends cheered when the two of them walked into the party together. Landon flashed a brief smile. The men pulled Todd into a huddle, congratulating him on a prize he hadn't won. She wiped the smile from her lips after hearing them slap hands and championing man. "That man went home and got his woman back," said Jay.

A shooting pain pierced through her heart and down her back. She shook it off and joined the ladies gathered around the love nest Tammy and McCaine created for the party.

Rose gold and off white decorum covered the closed in patio from the ceiling to the floor. Champagne bottles matching the candles and centerpieces on the tables illuminated the room, surrounded by all of the guests dressed in different shades of ivory and white. T&M trinkets added a personal touch of the couple of the hour, and Tammy was more than thrilled to tell the women all about the planning process.

"I saw a party like this online and knew this was how I wanted our place to look for this anniversary."

"You may have missed your calling," said Kim. "I'd hire you to be the visionary for my next party."

"Speaking of visionaries, Landon, you and Todd looked gorgeous as always walking in together. Does that mean you've called off the separation?" Tammy inclined.

"Jesus, men gossip more than women." Landon sighed.

"What separation?" Millicent looked at Landon.

"Tonight is not about me." Landon excused herself from the line of fire.

"Right." Tammy changed the subject. "Let me show you ladies tonight's party favors."

Tammy pulled out engraved copper mugs with metal straws. Kim inquired about the price, and McCaine's face wrinkled with strain.

"We don't talk about price, dear. McCaine would have an aneurysm if he knew."

Kim giggled at his reaction behind Tammy's back. She turned around and Kim changed the subject. "Has anyone heard from Jen?"

"I invited her, but never received a response."

Landon returned to the circle of women. "I went to see her recently. She's doing well down there. Jules couldn't attend tonight, so she sat this one out. She sends her love."

"So you've been communicating with people, just not with me," Millicent snided her. "I bet she knew of the separation."

Tammy cleared her throat. "Whatever's brewing between you two, don't hash it out at my party, but fix it before we go to Castillo Mas next week."

"Are we still doing that?" Landon frowned.

"Don't be a prude." Kim tapped her shoulder. "Everyone I know who's been to a voyeur club says it made their sex life even better."

Landon smirked. "And if you aren't having any trouble in that department, what good is it?"

"I don't know. Maybe spark new ideas."

"It's as if I don't know the women I have been friends with all these years." Landon rolled her eyes at Millicent. "Anyone else want a glass of champagne?" She left the ladies at the table.

"To be continued," Kim muttered.

Millicent pulled Jay away from the guys and wrapped his arms around her shoulders. They kissed and danced in the corner with every eye in the house studying their chemistry. Landon recognized she was in love, but couldn't see past their conflict to be happy for her. She wondered if jealousy played a part of her sudden detestation for the friend she's known her whole life. For their roles were reversing, and she would soon be alone.

Derailed

As she watched the new couple put on a show of affection from across the room, Todd was watching her. It inspired him to confess he was ready to come home. He walked over to her. "May I have this dance?" Landon gave him her hand. He held her close and whispered in her ear, "I see how you're looking at Mills. I once made you feel that way. I'd like to see you smile like that again. But for real, not for a show like those two spotlight whores." He and Landon chuckled cheek to cheek. Todd gazed into her eyes and squeezed her lower back. Landon felt the connection still between them. She resisted the tears bubbling in her eyes, spiraling on the inside of what she was about to lose. "I cried while you were gone. Waiting with my phone in my hand, hoping you would call. But you never did. It's why I moved out. It gave me time to realize the situation I put you in. And I'm sorry."

Landon hugged him tighter. "Let's not do this here."

"Tell me how to fix it. Us being at odds while those two of all people find love with each other. It's just not right. I'll never understand how that is working out and we're not."

"I'm against it, but I'm happy for them."

"I am too, but...."

"Honestly, it doesn't matter if we understand it."

"You're right again."

"Wanna know what bothers me the most about it?"

"Please. Tell me."

"That it could have been you over there with her."

Todd stopped dancing. "Not if she paid me."

Landon and Todd were so engrossed in their conversation, they didn't notice Millicent standing next to them.

She tapped Landon on the shoulder. "Can I borrow the Mrs. for a second?"

Todd waited for Landon's approval to let her go, leaned in, and whispered in her ear, "Not if she paid me."

They shared a quiet laugh.

"It would kill me." Landon pinched his cheek, then followed Millicent to the kitchen.

"You two don't look like you're separating to me. I see two people madly in love."

"We'll always love each other. Surely this isn't why you pulled me away?"

Millicent huffed. "What's going on between us?"

"I wish I knew. Things feel off since...you know."

"So I'm being punished for falling in love? I have to go at this alone. Not share how I feel with my best friend in the world? Because honestly, I need you right now."

"Why is that?"

"Because I'm terrified. Jay looks horrible on paper, but it frightens me how good it feels to be with him. I haven't felt this way in a long time."

"I'm happy for you. I truly am. I just can't help but wonder if you would do to me, what you've done to Jen. I'm finding it really hard to trust you all of a sudden. I'm sorry."

Tears formed in Millicent's eyes. She confessed, "I think about Jen every day. I'd love more than anything to repair our friendship. I regret hurting her. That was never my intention. But if I have to lose her to feel the way I feel with Jay, I'll do it. I wouldn't trade the happiness I feel for anything. Love has finally found me, and I'm not letting it go."

"And I hope it works out for you both."

"You do know I wouldn't do anything to hurt you. Not talking to you feels like I have lost a sister."

Landon looked at her, expressionless.

"So what have you been up to? Besides going to Miami?" Millicent continued to reach for a moment to bond.

Landon sensed her desperation. "I went home for a few days. Spent some time with my folks."

"How is everyone?"

"Everyone is well. I ran into Reynaldo while I was there."

"Did you?" Millicent's eyes grew wide.

"I dodged a bullet with that one. Tell you about that later."

"So you didn't?"

"God no. And I'm glad I didn't back then either."

Tammy intruded. "There you two are. Come. We're about to watch a video,"

After hours of dancing, eating, drinking, and viewing a slideshow of Tammy and McCaine over the years, Todd drove Landon home. The drive was quiet as old love songs played on the radio. So far he was two for two on his plan to show Landon she was the love of his life, and he would not go away easily. Now that the tone had been set, he hoped his final act to win her over was granted for the evening– Especially since Landon could be frisky when intoxicated.

Todd stroked the back of her hand as he walked her to the door. He held it up to his mouth, kissed the back of it, and got lost in Landon's eyes. He kissed her lips as they stood on the steps, praying for an invitation inside. Landon returned his advance, succumbing to desire by the minute. Todd's cock blossomed between them and she pulled back.

"I'm going to invite you in. But listen. No matter what happens, I want us to always be friends."

"I'll say what you want me to say if it gets me on the other side of that door, but I'd be lying if I said I could be your friend. I want to be your husband. Friends don't sound too good to me, baby."

"We love each other." Landon leaned in and placed her forehead against his.

Todd pulled her close and kissed her neck. "Baby, you are the only woman for me. The only woman I have eyes for. The only woman to get me excited like this."

"I want you just as bad, but promise me in the morning you'll go back to your place."

"I promise. I don't want to, but I will if that'll make you happy. Now, can I please have you?"

Landon led him to the top step. Todd pushed through the door, unwrapped his tie and threw his jacket to the floor. He lifted Landon's dress above her thighs. "You miss me laying pipe, don't you, baby?" He sighed in her mouth, then coiled his tongue with hers. With full desire bursting between them, he ripped her stockings to shreds, grinding against her on the wall below the staircase.

"Fix my plumbing, baby." Landon begged, stripping away his belt and unzipping his fly.

"Consider it done." Todd plunged inside her dripping walls. "Ahh," he groaned, biting his lower lip. "I'll leave my bill on the nightstand in the morning." He thrusted deep inside her pussy.

Landon wailed by his force, panting uncontrollably as the zipper on the back of her dress scratched her back. "Take this off," she whispered, lifting it above her head. Todd freed her and she elicited relief. He dipped between the line of her cleavage mounted like twin dome towers, unhooking her bra with the flick of a finger. His lips sucked her brown nipples until a rolling moan resounded from her throat. Lost in the sensation of his talented lips, she wound her aching pussy around his wand to the rhythm of his orchestrated tender jabs.

Every inch of Landon's cave vibrated. Todd reminded her how he knew to please her cravings, lifting her body up and down on his dick while his tongue traced her tanned skin from her bosom to her full lips. Familiar with her outline and corners, he stabbed her flesh side to side, making her slit sputter the warm cream he missed raining on him the past few weeks. "Daddy's home, baby." Todd pounded harder and stronger, drunk punching her walls until her come covered his dick completely and trickled down his legs. Wailing of ecstasy, Landon clutched her legs around him, enjoying the punishment of depriving him of her love for weeks. "That's my good girl. Show me you missed this dick. Cream for me, love. Ahh. You feel so fucking good," Todd groaned, lifting her legs above his shoulders. "I'm not finished with this good pussy yet."

He fucked Landon going up the stairs. Carrying her as she rode his stiff dick until they crash landed on the bed. Landon squealed at the painful pleasure of him ramming into her hole and grinding her fast, then slowing his strokes when he dug into his favorite corner at the top of her canal. He drilled until her legs weakened above him, trembling for more gluttonous punishment. He lifted his body and flipped Landon over on her stomach, kissing the center of her back down to her ass channel. "You've trickled all the way back here. Let me clean you up," he whispered, tonguing her dripped juices with tender strokes.

Landon gasped, "Oh! You nasty motherfucker."

"Mmm hmm," Todd moaned, prodding the center of her forbidden with circular motions.

Landon was destroyed, quavering uncontrollably. Todd failed to hold her still as she wiggled and wriggled at his mercy. He slowed down the pace, delicately kissing her back door, then smacked her ass and squeezed it like putty as he plowed his way back inside her warmth.

Strong, stiff and sturdy, he held his wood to the end of her fountain, pressing her clit with his thumb. Landon moaned. "I love it when you do that."

"I know you do," he said, rubbing her nub until she came again.

Todd joined her in exertion, holding her tight in his arms so she couldn't escape the perfect position her ass rested around his dick. He jolted in place, biting the back of her shoulder until his clip was empty.

They laid in their mess, still and contempt, listening to the insects trill outside the window, and the nightingale sing from the bush below their bedroom. Todd circled Landon's hair around his fingers.

"I was thinking we should go away. A change of scenery might do us some good."

"I just had a change of scenery, and it did do some good. Going away together will only further complicate things between us."

"After what just happened, you still want to separate?"

"Todd, remember the night of your mother's birthday party?"

"What does that have to do with us getting back together?"

"That phone call you received, how do you suppose that woman knew we were having problems?"

"I haven't given it much thought."

"I can think of two people. Either your mother has taken a liking to her, or your son ran back and told her about what he's heard. That's not the family I want to be a part of. I'm not fighting for your mother's attention or respect, and I don't want my business being shared with people in the street."

"Baby, I can't control what the boy tells his mother, or my mother's gossiping."

"That's my point. You and I aren't in control of us anymore. You and I have different paths now. It's why we have to end this. It's not going to work between us."

Todd kissed her good night, and fell asleep with her in his arms. He woke first as the rays of the sun graced him another morning next to the woman of his dreams. He watched her sleep for a short while, kissing her forehead while her hair found a way to tickle his nose each time he brushed it back. He lifted his sticky body from next to Landon's, and opened the drawer on his side of the bed. The notepad with The Jeffries printed across the

Derailed

top made him smile as he wrote Landon a note before keeping his word that he would leave in the morning.

> *Here is the bill for my service:*
> *Call me when you change your mind.*
> *I'll wait forever if I have to.*
> *T*

Chapter 18

The Empty Sea

Landon

It was weeks before Landon convinced herself to file the papers, but she persevered and hated herself for it. She couldn't bring herself to face Todd, ignoring his calls and late night visits sitting outside in the driveway. And when the files arrived with the date to finalize their decree, she read *Jeffries vs. Jeffries*, and grew physically ill.

Admitting to her mother she couldn't go through the process alone, Mother Davis and Launa surprised Landon the morning she was due in court.

"You don't have to go through with this, baby. Call it off. Todd has been praying you'll change your mind."

"Listen to Mama. Todd has been calling us night and day, begging us to convince you to change your mind," said Launa. "You are not going to find anyone better. I'm telling you, the sea is dryer than the desert."

"You both will hate me for saying this. Hell, I hate me for saying this. I can't be around that boy. And from what I've seen, he needs his father. This is best for everyone involved. Myself, Todd, and that boy. I have to walk away."

Todd refused to make eye contact with Landon when she entered the room. She stared at him, waiting for one final moment to look into his eyes and ask him to forgive her.

The lawyers mediated the terms of the agreement prior to their meeting, but Todd's lawyer stopped the proceedings to make an announcement. "My client has changed the terms of our previous agreement."

Landon tensed in her chair, still staring at Todd studying his phone below the table. Mr. Jeffries has agreed to give Mrs. Jeffries everything with the exclusion of his vehicles, his business, and partnership ventures with other parties. He is offering to relinquish any ownership of joint bank accounts, as well as his rights to the home on Mongrain Avenue, and continue to pay the mortgage while Mrs. Jeffries resides in the home, and gives full sale of profits to Mrs. Jeffries if, and, or when she decides to sell the property."

Landon's lawyer whispered with her, asking if she agreed to the changes. She wondered if his generosity was a final attempt to make her change her mind, and she called his name.

"Todd?"

He finally met eyes with her.

"Why are you doing this?"

Todd's lawyer interrupted. "Mr. Jeffries has also offered to pay off Mrs. Jeffries's vehicle if she agrees to abide by one request, submitted by Mr. Jeffries this morning."

"What is it?"

Landon's attorney intercepted. "Mrs. Jeffries, You hired me for a reason. I'll take it from here."

"My client requests that Mrs. Jeffries keep the last name Jeffries."

"Landon, do you agree to these terms?"

"Yes, unless I marry again." Landon added to the amendment.

Her attorney silenced her. "My client agrees to this request, and would like to add, pending upon a new marriage, she holds the right to remove the surname Jeffries at that time."

Landon signed the papers and stormed out of the hearing. She raced to the lobby and commanded Launa to get her out of there. Laura Lee stayed put, and waited for Todd to arrive at the exit.

"I'm sorry. You'll always be my son, and are still welcome in our house." She squeezed his hand. "You take care of that boy now."

"I will, but I'm not giving up on your daughter. If we have to do the whole wedding thing again, then so be it. These papers mean nothing to me. She's still my wife." Todd kissed Laura Lee on the cheek. "Love you, Ma."

Chapter 19

Sex Everywhere

Landon

Landon survived the first night as the former Mrs. Jeffries with the help of her mother and sister. Their company in the house kept her sane, but when they left the next morning, the shock set in. She struggled getting out of bed, her spirit was low, and her appearance staggered. The once sharp dresser switched to ill-fitting work attire with big jackets and flats, replacing her fitted dresses, skirts, and four inch heels.

As time went on, the house grew lonely, but Landon slowly worked her way out of the fog. Her circle kept her entertained, and for the one year anniversary of their visit to the sex club Castillo Mas, the ladies reassembled once again for a filthy night of voyeurism and fun.

They assembled at Kim's house. For an hour they lushed on homemade margaritas and wine before the limousine arrived to chauffeur them for the night.

"How the hell did we allow this one to drag us back to this place without the guys?" Tammy asked.

"Stop faking like you aren't happy the balls aren't dragging behind us this time." Kim slapped Tammy's leg. "This way we get to experience it freely. It's a girl's night!"

"Let's set some rules," Tammy suggested over the music. "No one get on that nasty ass bed in the middle of the floor, keep your feet on the floor, and come out of there with your panties on."

"What if we have a hall pass?" Kim teased.

All eyes shifted towards Kim.

"Did Brian give you the clearance tonight?" Tammy asked.

Kim blushed and looked at us up her nose. "Nah!" she shrieked. "I'm bullshitting y'all!"

Beyond the city limits they arrived at the house turned club, flashing red neon lights outside the heavily guarded gate. The chauffeur gave the security guards the password, and the gate opened.

"Y'all ready for a wild night?!" Kim fired up the squad.

"No turning back now." Landon sighed.

Kim passed a condom to Landon. "As the single lady in our group, you have clearance to do as you please. Just make sure you are protected."

Landon passed it back to her. "I'm good in that department."

"Somebody's got a maintenance man and been holding out." Kim raised her brows.

"Thank God." Millicent clapped her hands. "When do we meet this mystery man?"

Landon cleared her throat. "Shall we go inside?"

"And on that note, ladies, if you get uncomfortable or just not feeling the club, our driver has movies cued up, drinks, and snacks. Just come chill out in the car if need be until everyone is ready to leave. Hopefully that won't happen. Now let's go have a good time. Castillo Mas awaits!"

The club had been renovated since their first visit. Red lights flashed at the entrance as fog veiled the air. The laughter of the friends echoed between the slowed beats as they entered the first room, witnessing a naked woman in black spiked leather getting spanked on her exposed cheeks by two men licking wooden paddles.

Millicent whispered in Kim's ear. "How did you find this place?"

"We all have our little secrets, dear. You getting turned on already?"

"I don't need assistance in that department." Millicent turned up her nose.

As the lights switched from red to blue, and the fog cleared the passageway to the next exhibit, the ladies entered a foreplay room. Participants on a stage, some fully naked, others half dressed, pleasured their lovers for voyeurs circling the room, holding up rating cards. They watched a woman deepthroat a seven inch dick, receiving a perfect score of ten by the judges, and a man eat the pussy of a woman until her torso fell off of the table as she balanced and spread wide with his face planted up her ass.

"Give him a ten too!" Kim shouted.

"Give her the ten for balance." Millicent chuckled.

"We have been in this room for twenty minutes," Landon pointed out.

"Seriously?" Tammy's eyes twirled.

Landon showed the girls the time on her phone.

"Damn. Then give all of them a ten for holding people's attention," Tammy joked. "Y'all ready to move on?"

"Yeah," they mumbled.

As they trekked down the hall, the lights went out, and the music stopped. Neon arrows blinked on the wall, guiding them ahead into a gold room with a woman chained in a stirrup machine with cables connected to her breast.

"This is so much better than the last time we came," Landon

said. "These exhibits make it more of an experience than horny people fucking in a room."

"I agree. I was prepared to be bored." Tammy laughed.

Buzz, electrical shocks stimulated the model's breasts. She shook and hollered, then smiled of delight. A man walked onto the stage with a purple dildo in his hand and placed it inside the front of her panties. It vibrated against her as she begged him to turn it up higher. He zapped her breasts again with the push of a button on the machine, then gripped her face. "I give the orders," he said, then licked the side of her face.

"Okay, I'm gonna head to the next room. This one is a bit much for me." Tammy squeezed through the group.

"Wait," said Kim.

"Ah!" the woman screamed and shivered on stage uncontrollably.

"I'm a little intrigued," Millicent confessed.

"Then you stay and watch this shit." Tammy led the way out.

The fog grew thicker as the gold room faded behind them. Down the murky hallway, they grew silent until the arrows pointed them inside a dark room where the lights flashed from wall to wall every two seconds. The ladies held hands, ensuring they stayed together in this room. With every flicker of light a couple appeared to surround them, engaged in a random sex act. Their heads turned like they were watching a tennis match. Left to right they were stunned by men on women, women on women, two men on one woman, and countless other arrangements shown only when the light flashed on each wall.

"Which way out of this room?" Landon whispered.

"I don't know. I'm scared to move and end up in the mix." Tammy giggled.

"This way." Kim led them.

Slow music played ahead with a purple haze clouded above.

Derailed

A hostess holding wrist bands stood at the entrance next to a security guard with a nightstick.

"Read the rules for entering this room." She pointed to a sign on the wall behind her.

- *All are allowed to enter.*
- *You may look.*
- *You may touch.*
- *To participate, you must wear this band as your form of consent.*
- *Do not take off the band while in this room.*
- *Doing so will result in removal from the property.*

All of their heads peeked into the room of moans and groans from sex crazed party goers going at it like beasts in the wild. A man fingered for them to come inside while he fucked a woman from behind.

"I'll pass," said Landon. "I don't want to be touched by none of these people"

"We all will," said Millicent. "How do we get to the bar?"

"Speak for yourself." Kim held out her wrist. "I'll see y'all in a few."

The hostess pointed to the door on the left. "Follow the stairs. Bar is down below."

Bass pounded louder than the music from the other rooms as they entered a neon blue room with a pool sitting in the corner opposite of the bar.

"Welcome to the pool party of your dreams," said a hostess welcoming them inside.

"I'm in the wrong business," said Tammy.

"I want to dance." Millicent shook her hips to the music.

"I'll join you two later. I need a drink. That was a lot to take in." Landon headed to the bar.

The bar area was filled with regulars that immediately noticed the newbie. Thirsty hounds surrounded her as she searched for an opening to place her order, while Tammy and Millicent were crowded by dirty dancing rejects. A man offered Landon his seat at the bar.

"What's your poison?"

"Strawberry daiquiri."

"That's Kool-Aid."

"That's what I want."

"Get the lady a strawberry daiquiri," he ordered. "It's on me, pretty lady."

"Thanks, but I can manage to buy myself a drink. I appreciate the offer though."

"I'm sure you can. What brings you to a place like this?"

"Bachelorette party," Landon lied.

"Oh. Someone is getting taken off the market. I hope it isn't you."

Landon looked at her naked ring finger and rubbed it.

"Not yet."

"So, what's your name?"

"Lashika."

"Nice to meet you, Lashika." He leaned in her ear. "I know that's not your real name, but I love role playing."

Landon moved her head away from his and paid for her drink. The man placed a twenty dollar bill in front of her and told the bartender to keep them coming. He leaned in towards her again and whispered," There's more where that came from. How much to leave your friends behind for the night and come home with me."

"Sir, I am not a hooker. Have a good night."

Derailed

"Tell me your price, and I'll raise it."

Landon rolled her eyes and took her drink to the dance floor. She grooved with Millicent and Tammy, giving them a laugh at her weak offer at the bar.

"At least you know you still got it," said Tammy.

"Please. That man would go home with the first woman who says yes." Landon laughed.

"Guys, I have a question. Who told the guys we were coming here?"

Landon and Tammy followed Millicent's eyes to a table above the pool area.

"Them being here has Brian written all over it." Tammy shook her head.

Chapter 20

What's Mine Is Mine

Todd

On an upper level deck above the pool, the smell of marijuana perfumed the air. One by one the men at the table took a toke from fat rolled cigars, ending in the hands of McCaine.

"You can't hit this. Your job has random testing." Jay snatched it from his hands.

"I don't need you to babysit me. I'm grown," McCaine argued.

"Go ahead and be grown and unemployed then. Don't ask me to pay your bills either, bruh," Jay snapped.

"Okay, okay. I'll pass. I'm going to get another drink. This round is on the babysitter." McCaine held out his hands.

Jay passed McCaine a Franklin. "Keep the change for the next round too, errand boy."

McCaine ogled a couple of half naked women making out on the stairs on his way to the bar. He worked his way through the horde and placed an order for four beers, noticing his wife, Landon, and Millicent near a crowd of men chanting, "Shots!" at the end of the bar. He moseyed back to the table and reported to the men, "Brian was right. They're here."

"Ain't this 'bout a bitch. Coming to a place like this without us. What the fuck was Kim thinking?" Brian stuck out his chest.

"What are they doing?" Jay searched the crowd.

"Shots with a bunch of jerkoffs."

"Do they look drunk?" Brian asked.

"I didn't see Kim down there. Tammy is nearly blitzed. Millicent might not be too far behind."

"And Landon?" Todd asked.

"She's lit." McCaine shook his head.

"I don't care what dummy buys Tammy's drink. I'm still recovering from that damn party."

"Alright, fellas. It's been a fun night. Time to go shut this shit down." Jay led them to the bar area.

They wormed through the crowd, separating to find the party girls. Brian stood by as Kim whipped her hair around, dancing risque in a sandwich between two men on the dance floor below a shadow from the balcony. Jay crept up behind Millicent.

"You don't belong in a place like this."

Millicent faced him and laughed. "Who blabbed?"

"It don't matter."

"You mad?"

"Nah."

"Then shut up and dance with me."

"I only do that at the house."

Todd tapped Millicent. "Where's Landon?"

"She was right next to me."

Todd searched through the crowd with a glint of desperation in his eyes. He spotted Brian and Kim laughing on the dance floor, Tammy and McCaine raising hell on one end of the bar, and Jay and Millicent on the steps wrapped in each other's arms. He forced his way through the crowded bar and scowled at the

Derailed

faces of men glaring at him until he landed eyes on Landon having a conversation with Dario Powers.

He walked up on them and stared at Landon talking to Dario more than he could handle. She felt his eyes burning her back, turned her head full of hair around, and locked eyes with him. She would never get the look on his face out of her mind. It was endearing and passionate and angry. It made her feel like a villain for pulling the plug on their love, and selfish for placing her happiness before their bond. It also made her feel guilty for the way she mishandled herself with Dario at work, even though they were no longer man and wife, and she never crossed the line with him.

Todd smiled at her and she felt at ease. Glossy-eyed and grinning, she smiled back at him and lowered her head with rosy cheeks glowing like a blood moon. In her drunkenness she revealed to Dario she was now divorced, and he used that information to rile up Todd.

He placed his hand around her waist and stared Todd up and down, grinning at the anger raging in his face. Todd pushed Dario's shoulder. "Don't fucking play with me, man. You ain't 'bout that life. You ain't learn your lesson last time?" Todd barked, then knocked his hand from Landon's waist.

"She ain't yours no more," Dario taunted him.

"She'll always be mine." Todd stood in his face, clenching his fist so tight the muscles in his biceps amplified.

Dario smirked. "I knew the moment your hood ass showed up to my house it was only a matter of time before you lost her. A woman like this has no business with ghetto trash like you."

Landon stood at Todd's side. "What's he talking about?"

"Landon, go over by the stairs with Jay and Mills."

"No baby. You stay over here with a real man." Dario reached for Landon's hand.

Todd smacked it away. The people standing near them at the

bar grabbed their drinks and left. He stepped to his left, shielding Landon behind him. "Landon, get from over here," Todd ordered. She listened this time. "If you think for one minute I'm going to let you put Landon in the middle of your bigamist shit, you got another thing coming."

"It must suck to have a woman like that leave you. Baby girl is good and liquored up, and was all smiles over here until you showed up. But that's cool. I have forty hours with her through the week. We'll send you a wedding invitation."

The clenched fist at Todd's side rose to the air. The anguish, humiliation, regret, sorrow, and frustration he kept hidden inside flowed through the blood rushing to his head, and veered to his fist as he knocked Dario with a sweet punch to the jaw.

Dario held his lip and smiled. "I have witnesses this time."

"Fuck your witnesses." Todd sucker punched him in the nose.

Blood dripped from Dario's nostrils, splattering on his shirt and to the floor. Rumbling of the crowd rushing towards the exit, and creaks of chairs sliding across the floor muffled Dario shouting at Todd when he sneak attacked him with a glass full of beer to the head. Todd remained composed and checked for blood where the glass broke above his ear. Splotches of beer drenched the sleeve of his shirt. He glared at Dario with the eye of a tiger, and grabbed him by the back of his shirt as he attempted to flee from the bar. Todd slammed his head on the back of a wooden stool. "I told you to stay away from my fuckin' wife!" He repeated as he pounced on top of Dario, beating him to the floor until security bum rushed him.

Dario rose to his feet with the help of a few bystanders and security. He wiped the blood from his lip, closely watching the other security officers rough house Todd. When the grip of one of the security team holding him up loosened, he broke free and snuck a blow to Todd's stomach while he was heavily constrained with both of his arms above his head.

"She's fair game now! It's over for you!" He laughed, spitting out blood.

Jay caught Dario from behind and jabbed him in his ribs. Security lost control of the situation and hemmed up Jay while Todd freed himself from their restraint. He snaked between the chaos and clobbered Dario with a one-two combination. Dario leaned forward. He held his stomach, stumbling like a drunk, then patted his eye. Todd caught him again and stunned his other eye.

The crowd dispersed into chaos. Dario swung punches in every direction, landing an accidental blow to Todd's eye, but in turn was hit with a wind up uppercut to his chin, weakening his knees, and laying him flat on his back. Todd kicked Dario until he curled up into a ball between two stools.

Security grabbed Todd and threw him and Jay out the back door of the club. They fled to the side of the building, blending in with the staff gathered by the employee entrance smoking cigarettes. They eased their way to Jay's car, slid inside and called the girls.

Jay: I'm parked by the gate. Bring Landon with you.

We've left the lot. Stuck in this traffic. :Mills

Jay: Pull over at the first exit and wait for me.

Okay. :Mills

The gang met at the gas station at the first exit off the highway. Todd walked over to the limousine, led Landon out by the hand, and sat with her in the back of Jay's car.

"I'm not apologizing. Do you see what I would do for you?"

Landon shook her head yes.

"Promise me you won't ever have anything to do with the likes of that guy."

"You don't have to worry about that. I don't fancy him."

"And I believe you. Because I love you. I'll always love you."

"I know."

"How you been?" He grabbed her hand.

"Okay. I have my days." She smiled at her hand inside of his.

"Still the prettiest girl in the room."

Landon looked up and gazed into his eyes. Todd licked his lips and leaned in to taste hers as Tammy knocked on the car window.

"Todd what the hell was that? You need to work on that temper, boy. Landon, can we get out of here?"

She waved her hand. "You guys go ahead. Tell Kim I'll pick up my car tomorrow."

Tammy grinned at the look in Landon's eyes. "Talk some sense into slugger here."

Jay returned to the car with Millicent, cranked it, and merged into traffic. Millicent turned around with her arm posed against the headrest, smiling at Todd and Landon having a moment.

"What got into you, Todd?" She grinned.

"Millicent, not now." Landon sternly glared at her.

"You didn't need to beat that poor man like that. Landon has never liked him."

Derailed

Jay tapped Millicent's leg. "Baby, it's been handled. Let's just stay out of it."

"What was all that stuff you were saying in the club about learning his lesson the last time?" Landon asked.

Todd stuttered. "A while back I had him investigated when he was harassing you. I found out some devious things he's involved in, and warned him not to get you caught up in the middle of his mess. But don't worry about any of that. Just promise you'll stay away from him."

"I promise."

"Yeah, Landon. Stop dangling that string on my boy's head and getting him into shit. You know you still love him. Quit fuckin' around." Jay fussed.

"I know you ain't talking after you broke up a friendship. Somebody needs to put a foot up your ass."

Jay stared at Landon and Todd in the rearview mirror. "T. Since when your girl talk like that?"

Todd chuckled and shrugged his shoulders. "I'on know, but I like it." He grinned, kissing the back of Landon's hand.

Jay grinned at Landon. "I hear you, Sis. Message received. I won't fuck up this time. I give you my word. I'm in love with Mills." He called Millicent over and kissed her on the side of his mouth as he drove. " I love you, girl."

Millicent smiled. "Love?"

"You heard me."

Jay swerved on the road as he attempted to maul Millicent's face with one hand on the wheel, and the other caressing her chin. Todd and Landon chastised him to cut it out. "Pull over," said Millicent, pulling on his shirt collar, kissing his cheek. The car slowed down and veered off at the next exit, stopping in the safety lane in front of the stop sign. Jay turned off the engine and tackled Millicent.

"That place got you turned on, I see," he mumbled.

"And you just said you love me." Millicent sighed.

Todd and Landon watched them go at it, squirming in the back seat.

"I don't think they're coming up for air." Landon joked.

"I remember the last time we were like that."

Landon's eyes grew big.

"What's it been? Two, almost three months?" Todd stared at her with his teeth sinking into his bottom lip.

Millicent gasped and pushed Jay back. She sat up and turned towards Landon. "Todd is the maintenance man!"

"You ain't know that?" Jay scowled.

"You knew and didn't tell me?" Millicent complained.

Landon whispered to Todd, "You told him?"

"He figured it out on his own." Todd smiled on the side of his mouth.

Todd grabbed Landon by her thighs and pulled her body closer to his. His eyes tempted her as they gazed deep into hers, coaxing her to stop fighting the urge he sensed growing inside of her. Their lips finally locked in a tender, sensual kiss as Jay and Millicent cheered them on.

Todd lowered his back against the door, sliding down to the seat. He pulled Landon with him, then waved for Jay to turn around and give them privacy.

Jay and Millicent returned to their own desires, giving into the heat firing between them. They opened their eyes and snickered at the sound of Todd's zipper coming undone, and held their laughs when Landon's lips smacked around Todd's pipe.

Todd, unable to grunt silently and control the passionate sighs of Landon's lip service, held up his hand and waved for Jay to get out of the car. The door slammed and Todd moaned, "Baby, can I come home!" softly massaging Landon's scalp as she filled her mouth with his dick, holding her gag as his hips pressed forward. "Hop on top before I bust," Todd ordered.

Derailed

Landon's quivering legs climbed on top of him, and the car rocked side to side. Millicent hopped on the trunk, her breasts jiggling from the motion. Jay kissed the cushion of her pillows bouncing under the moonlight, and pulled out his penis. He rubbed it on Millicent's leg. "You trust me?" he asked, sliding her thong to the side. Jay's arrogance and imperiousness overpowered Millicent's detestation for him, and brought out a wild desire she hadn't felt for some time. She nodded and spread her legs wider, then held on to his shoulders as he stroked his dick with his hands and coached his tip between her southern lips.

The car squeaked and shook from the throttling of Landon working Todd over on the inside and Jay pressing Millicent's ass up and down the edge of the car on the outside. Landon contained her squeals, huffing as Todd long-dicked her from below, rolling her supple ass around his cock. With a glimmer in his eyes, he traced the lines of her mouth, worshiping her while she took command of his vigorous thrashing.

Outside, Jay would not be outdone. Roughly, he fucked Millicent in the dewy night air, making her scream into his shoulders. The excitement of being seen by passersby made her feel like the models in the exhibits at the club. She grinned as Jay put on his own display with beating hearts between them, racing to the finish line.

The car settled, and the couples headed back to the city with the music blasting and not a word spoken between them. Jay dropped Todd off at Landon's house, and the former lovers carried on for days, unable to break the soul tie that bound them. "Baby, what are we doing?" Todd begged for the answer he desperately wanted to hear. Landon never gave it to him. She kept quiet, accepting they couldn't go on like this for much longer.

"I'm confused. I have to let you go, but I can't."

"This is fuckin' with my head, baby. We always had great sex, but since we've been sneaking around, I want you more than ever. I want to come home."

"This is all my fault. I should have never reached out to you."

"I'm glad you did." He held her hand.

"I should have let you move on with your life. Can you forgive me?"

"There's nothing to forgive. But we gotta fix, whatever this is. I can't keep going on like this. I want my wife back."

Chapter 21

Seasons change

Jen

Summer came to an end, and it was time for Max to leave fun in the sun and return to Detroit. Jen stayed with Landon for the week, caught in the adventures of Todd's midnight visits, and intense conversations between him and Landon when it was time for him to say goodbye.

She interrupted them one night, and asked for a moment alone with Todd. Landon was relieved the departure wasn't going to be torturous for once.

"I need a favor from you, Todd."

"What you need?"

"Has Jay mentioned anything about full custody?"

"I don't know if I need to get in the middle of that, Jen."

"Look, I want to have a sit down with him, but he's vague whenever I ask him, and I just need an idea of how he'll react if I file for full custody."

"All I know is he was excited Max was coming home this week, and he talked about him the whole time he was away."

"I just want my son to be happy. And I don't know if he's happier here, or with me. It's hard to tell. Being that you are going through your own father/son thing right now, I thought I'd ask your opinion."

"I feel that. All I can tell you is, have the conversation. It's been a minute, and you both seem happy, so let all that past shit go, and work it out. You see I'm still trying."

Jen squeezed Todd's hand. "And don't give up. I think you're wearing her down."

Jen took Todd's advice and arranged for Jay to meet with her for lunch on The Jeffries' back lawn. Jay arrived ready for a battle with his smug face in tow.

"You can put that away today," Jen said, opening the door.

"What you talking about, girl?"

"That look. I didn't invite you over to argue. Leave the hostility outside." Jen welcomed him into the house.

Jay stepped inside and they stared at each other. "It's good to see you too, stranger."

"Todd and Landon are out back. Shall we?"

He followed her to the deck. "Looking good, Jen." He clicked his teeth.

Jen shook her head. "Thank you. I see some things haven't changed."

"You'd be surprised."

They sat with the divorced couple like old times, staring at one another around the table.

"I'm just going to say it. This has to be the most bizarre luncheon I've ever attended." Jay joked. "It's like we traveled back in time or something. You got L & T sitting over there divorced, but carrying on like they're not, and us." Jay pointed to himself and Jen. "What is this about?"

"About mending our friendship and keeping the circle tight. It's been a strange, difficult year. Wouldn't you agree?" Jen asked.

"I do."

"And we need to fix that. I asked you over today because I don't want to hate you anymore."

"What about Millicent?"

"Let me deal with that in my own time. My main concern is you. Our issues are starting to affect Max. We both want custody. Neither of us is going to budge, so we need to work something out better than we have right now."

"What do you propose?"

"Split custody six months of the year."

"Sorry, Jen, but no. I think you should move back to Detroit. You do that, and I'll agree he can live with you, while I'm still active in his life. I don't trust another man raising him full time. No disrespect to your boy toy."

"His name is Julian."

"Yeah, him. I'm the one responsible for helping Max become a man. I don't know that cat like that."

Jen sighed.

"You know what I can do for him and will do for him. It was hard enough letting him come down for the summer without seeing him."

"The travel is starting to wear thin, Jay. On me and him."

"So move back."

"And a part of me felt like he was distant with me. I could tell he missed you and that hurts me. He's sad, and I'm starting to feel like I'm not enough anymore."

"A mother can never be replaced, Jen." Jay assured her.

"So if I stopped coming up as often as I have this past year, you won't poison him against me?"

"Never dat."

"And...stop him from calling someone else Mama."

"Is that what this is really about?" Jay frowned at Jen. "Max would never call another woman your name. I won't allow it. You gotta trust me."

"It would kill me, Jay. And make sure you tell him I called and I love him every day. Even if I don't. Tell him."

"I give you my word." Jay squeezed her hand.

"Then that's settled. You and I no longer need to argue over custody, and we can work on becoming friends again."

"Jen, don't get me wrong, I'm happy we finally settled on this, but I gotta know. What changed your mind?"

Jen looked at Landon. "There are some things I will share with you at a later date. As of right now, you're the stable one and what's best for him."

"I don't buy it." Jay huffed.

"Everything is fine. Jules offered to transfer to the league here, so I could be closer to Max, but I just opened my makeup bar and need to see a profit before opening a second here."

"I have the cash if you want it." Jay looked at Todd. "If that will get you back here to be with our son, T and I will both invest."

"I need to discuss that with Jules."

"For what? He hasn't married you yet."

"He has a point," Landon added.

"Men don't think with their heart like women. We think with our head," said Jay.

"Which one?" Jen snickered.

Jay buried his head beneath his hands and laughed. "I know that low blow was directed at me, and good one. I'll give you that." He clapped his hands, flicking a toothpick from side to side in his mouth. "I had that coming."

Jen raised her brows. "Accountability. That's new."

"Do you want this money to start this business or not, 'cause you talking rather slick."

"I should be allowed as many as I want. Don't you think?"

Jay was humbled. He looked at Jen down his nose and showed all of his teeth before holding up his hands and nodding.

"I'm the bad guy. That'll never change, but I have to admit. I missed this. I miss you. Aside from what I did and am doing, we had a good time together until my shit caught up to me. But I like being able to talk to you like this."

"Then let's build on that."

"Agreed." Jay reached for her hand.

Jen shook it, then smacked it away. "One more thing. You, Max, and I need to go out for dinner before I leave so he can see we are getting along."

"And what about...?"

Jen silenced Jay before he uttered the words. "You, me, and our son. Capiche?"

"Got it."

"Now, go pick up my son and bring him to see his mama."

"Yes, ma'am. Think hard about that business proposal. Me and Todd are always down to make a little money."

Chapter 22

Fall leaves

todd

Autumn turned the green leaves to orange, yellow, and red and plummeted them to the ground in time for the annual Dine & Drink Festival. Todd hadn't heard from Landon in a month. When she didn't call to confirm they would be attending the event together, he arrived solo, surprised to see Landon already sitting amongst the group.

Her energy was off. Her greeting was cold, and he couldn't help but notice how it seemed intentional she was seated at the end of the table when two chairs were available at the opposite end. He sat across from Jay, leaving the seat open between him and Tammy.

"That finally stopped..." Jay eluded in code.

"Seems so." Todd poured the wine in front of him into the empty glass. "Jen send that proposal?"

"Got it this morning. I'll bring it by your place tomorrow."

"Cool."

Todd glanced at Landon, searching for the right moment to say hello. All night they stared at each other, turned away, and stole looks when the other wasn't watching. By the end of the night, they found their moment, and took a walk away from everyone. A light breeze blew Landon's hair wild with the wind. The night air drew them close. Todd stood with his hands in his pockets. His elbows brushed against her sweater, tempted by her icy rose scent the swirling draft perfumed in the air.

"How you getting home?"

"I drove." Landon sipped her last drip of wine.

"How many glasses have you had?"

"Shit, I can't remember. But I'm good."

"How about I follow you to make sure?"

"As much as I want to say yes, I'm going to have to pass tonight."

"What, scared your boyfriend is going to see you with the likes of me?" Todd teased.

A curve formed on the side of her mouth. "No boyfriend. Just being smarter."

"Is that even possible?"

"Todd..."

"Have we actually arrived at the end of the road?"

"I think so. Sneaking around has been nice. Really nice. But I found myself becoming attached to you. Craving you more and more, and that has to stop. It's time we both move on."

"I knew this was coming. The one time I wish I was wrong."

"I wish I was too."

Todd exhaled sharply. "So the last time was the last time?"

"I'm afraid so. I better get going. You take care of yourself."

"Shit, I'll try."

Against Landon's wishes, Todd followed her home. He watched her pull into the garage and waited for the bedroom light to turn on, then made his way home in disbelief they were officially Mr. and Mrs. No More.

Chapter 23

Some Getting Used To
Landon

The snow fell early in October, dusting the city with a warning of one of the coldest winters to come. By November, one inch turned into three, then four inches as the brutal cold settled into the Midwest, forcing travel plans to delay, and loved ones to be missed for the holiday.

Tammy always held a huge Thanksgiving feast at her house, but with the rumor mill circling Todd was back out on the dating scene, Landon chose to host her family at her home. They piled in from Flint, helping her decorate for the holidays, and change her home's appearance. The old was out, and the new arrived for days with delivery men in and out with furniture and appliances.

The pictures on the wall were updated, the frames new in color, and accented corners with deep hues of auburn and caramel toned the house, making it warm and inviting for the season. The changes made her feel better about her single life, and the presence of her family livened up her spirits, serving as the perfect distraction for the loneliness looming above her at night.

With Jules traveling with the team, Jen arrived on Thanksgiving Eve with Max at her hip.

"I couldn't let you spend the first holiday of this season alone," she said.

"You are a sight for sore eyes. Come in. I want you to meet my family."

"I should have called. I feel like I'm intruding."

"Not at all. You being here is perfect. I was afraid my nephew was going to be bored out of his mind, but he and Max can keep each other entertained in Todd's old mancave. He already has a video game set up in there."

"Can I go, Mama?"

Jen tapped his shoulders. "Yes and be nice."

"Yes ma'am."

The lonely house was suddenly the lively house, full for the long weekend with good company and loving vibes. And though Laura Lee's words were eating her alive, "You're going to run him into another's woman's arms," she accepted her fate and dodged any further conversation about Todd. But Laura Lee wasn't easily fooled. When everyone spoke what they were thankful for during Thanksgiving dinner, she knew Landon was hurting.

"You girls should get out of the house. I'll keep watch of the boys with the help of your father. Go out. Be young."

"The clubs in the city are pretty fun during the holidays." Jen suggested.

"You don't have to ask me twice. I'm game." Launa kissed her mother's cheeks. "I'll be ready in twenty."

Plowed snow lined the salted, cleared streets, and the downtown night sky lit the mood. The ladies popped into the latest rave, stuck in a long line of partygoers. The wind blew so strong, the temperature felt ten below.

"I can't feel my toes anymore." Landon shivered.

"Fuck this. I'm going to wait in the car." Jen ran off.

Derailed

Launa and Landon followed.

"I have an idea. Let's skip the club, and go warm up at one of those Spanish Coffee Houses that sells those nose warmer drinks with live acts."

"I know just the place," said Jen, driving them to a late night café near the dealership where she once worked.

They piled inside a booth and found more than music and warm drinks. A group of friends were seated next to them and struck a decent conversation. Against the owner's wishes, they slid their table closer to the booth, keeping the girls laughing and entertained while the night's act sang slower, softer renditions of the most popular songs. "I know this one!" Launa shouted, singing the tune loudly from the audience.

"You girls want to do something fun?" the husky one asked.

"We don't know your names." Launa pointed out.

"I'm Caleb, this is Seth, and this is Coran."

They saluted the ladies.

"I was going to suggest we get out of here and go ice skating in Martius Park."

"Isn't it closed at this hour?" Landon asked.

"So, we'll have it all to ourselves."

They followed the gentlemen, stoned and glossy-eyed. Bundled up like snowmen, they snuck into the park, and slid around on the ice like kids without skates until the wind gusts became too heavy. The guys escorted them to their car. Landon and Jen sat inside, warming the engine and defrosting their hands against the vents, watching Launa put the moves on Caleb.

"It's hard to believe you two came from the same woman," said Jen.

Launa hopped in the car..

"You get that, Little Sis?" Landon teased.

"Was there any doubt I would?" Launa laughed.

Early in the morning, the aroma of a famous Laura Lee breakfast woke the house. She put on a pot of coffee, fried sausages and eggs, baked biscuits and griddled pancakes for the boys.

"Girls!" Laura Lee woke them, passed out in their rooms. "Get up and go eat. I want you to take me to catch the sales."

"Ma, you could have mentioned that before you told us to go out and get shitfaced," Launa complained.

"I know you didn't catch a suitor with that mouth. Get up. Let's not waste the day."

Jen tiptoed into Landon's room after Laura Lee woke her. She keeled over laughing in Landon's bed.

"Your mother just woke me up and told me what I was going to do today. I have never had a mother do that. I love her so much."

"She set us up."

"That's what Launa said." Jen cackled. "I love the shadiness of it all."

Papa Davis gave his word to keep an eye on the boys while the women shopped, grabbed lunch, shopped some more, and ran into Millicent in the food court of the mall.

"Fancy seeing you girls here. Hello, Mother Davis." Millicent kissed her cheeks and hugged her. "How are you?"

"Doing good. Having a blast with my girls. And you, dear?"

"I'm doing well. How is Pops?"

"He's at Landon's with the boys." Laura Lee noticed Jen and her girls rolling their eyes at Millicent. "Well, it was good seeing you. Hope it's not so long next time."

"You too."

"Girls, I'll be sitting over here while one of you grabs that fancy latte drink for me." Laura Lee tightened her lips at her girls as she excused herself.

Millicent glanced over Jen and questioned Landon. "Why didn't you tell me your family was in town?"

Derailed

"Time got the best of me. You wouldn't believe how exhausted I am."

"The holidays, right. Well maybe we'll catch up at Kim's game night, or are you not coming to that as well?"

"We're definitely coming to game night." Launa smirked.

"Good. Well, see you all there."

Millicent walked off, confused why Launa rolled her eyes at her. She waved at Laura Lee, then looked back at the ladies whispering amongst themselves.

"We're not going to game night. It's always couples, and I don't want to see Todd's new fling." Landon crossed her hands.

"Yes, we are, and it's going to be epic." Launa snapped her fingers.

"I'm with Landon. I'd feel better if Jules was with me."

"You two need to learn how to chill. Like me. I've got this under control." Launa grinned.

"What aren't you telling us?" Landon narrowed her eyes at her sister.

"Caleb and his friends want to hang tonight. He'll bring his friends, and we'll show up, ruffle a few feathers, start some ruckus, win some money, and be out. Besides, don't you both want to watch everybody get uncomfortable when we walk through the door?"

Jen laughed out loud. "Why hasn't your sister hung out with us before?"

"This is exactly why."

Chapter 24

Game, Set, Match

launa

'*F*unky fresh dressed to impress ready to party*'*, Launa riled up Jen and Landon with her blend of throw-your-phone hip hop hits. With *Ante Up* blasting through her speakers, she and Jen bonded, shaking their hair and nodding their heads while Landon remained prim and proper in the backseat, nervous about seeing Todd with another woman on his arm.

They swung by the grocery store closest to Kim and Brian's neighborhood to meet the trio from the café. Smoke seeped through the cracked window of Caleb's car, signaling he would follow them to the party.

He and Launa hugged when they got out of their cars. Jen and Landon watched them bond, huddled together on the sidewalk.

"Your friends getting out or what?" Launa asked.

"Yeah, we just weren't expecting to be led to a neighborhood like this. We didn't take y'all for bougie people last night."

Launa laughed. "My sister is the bougie one. This is her friend's house, and I assure you they are a little bougie, but mostly cool people. I promise we'll have a good time."

"I am not bougie." Landon mugged Launa on her way inside the house.

"Shee-it." Launa swiped at her, snickering with Jen behind Landon's back. "She knows she is. She just doesn't like to hear it," Launa whispered to Caleb and Jen walking on each side of her. "Caleb, tell Seth and Coran to get out of the car."

Caleb waved to the guys. "It's cool."

Fashionably late, the odd mix entered Kim and Brian's house. The chatter silenced and all eyes shifted to Landon, Jen, and Launa walking in with three strange men behind them.

"The fuck is this?" Brian mumbled.

"It's about time you got here. And you brought dates." Kim's voice went south. "Great. The more the merrier."

"Yeah. More suckas to lose their money!" McCaine shouted.

"Ignore him. I'm Kim, this is my husband Brian, and welcome to our home."

Landon spoke. "Kim and Brian, you've met my sister Launa before I'm sure, and these are our new friends, Caleb, Seth, and Coran."

"Nice to meet you all. Come on in, put your coats over there, and let the games begin." Kim smiled nervously, then pulled Landon to the side. "You vouch for these people?"

"Right now, yes. But if something pops off, blame my sister." Landon raised her brows and made her way into the living room.

"What's up, everybody? Who was in here screaming about losing money? I'm ready to get in that ass! Sup, Bruh-law?" Launa leaned down so Todd could kiss her cheek.

"Winning so far."

"Not for long." McCaine slammed his cards on the table.

"You must be the shit talker," said Launa. "I have my eye on you."

As the night started with a serious game of poker, Launa sat on the sidelines, peeping at who was the real competition. Todd

Derailed

and Landon glimpsed at each other for the first hour, smirking with one another about Launa increasing the awkward vibe in the room.

"We are not playing poker all night. Save that for when you all meet up at Jay's house or something." Kim stared at Brian.

"Let this be the last hand, so we can play whatever Kim has on her list." Brian folded his hand. "But make no mistake, we will end the night at the card table."

"Time for Trivia, everyone!" Kim announced.

"We already know who the smartest person is in the room. Do we really need to play this?" McCaine pointed to himself.

As the game proceeded, tension began to build thanks to Launa's shenanigans. Whenever Todd answered a question correctly, she shouted, "Alright Bruh-law!" Landon tapped her a few times when she thought no one was looking, but Jen saw it every time and couldn't contain her laughter.

Todd's date allowed the dig to roll off of her back the first few times, but the more Launa ignored her presence, the more she lost her patience and decided to speak up. "Hi. I'm Shanice. I don't think we've been introduced."

"We haven't, but I'm sure you know my name by now. Everyone in here has it on their tongue. Ain't that right loser...I mean, McCaine." Launa snickered.

"Landon, get your sister please." McCaine held up praying hands.

"Todd told me about the others, but I'm afraid he didn't mention anything about you, Launa."

"I ain't the one you need to be worried about." Launa chuckled. "Caleb, baby, can you bring me a beer and keep me warm? It's a bit chilly where I'm sitting."

Jen looked at Landon, and they smirked. Jay saw Landon and Jen communicating across the room. He leaned over to Landon and said, "Your little sister is feisty."

"You like that don't you, Jay?" Launa winked at him.

Millicent cleared her throat.

Launa turned to Jay and smiled. "My bad. I didn't mean to get you in trouble. I thought I was about to be your flavor for the week."

Todd giggled. "Yooo Launa. Chill, Sis."

"I'm just playing around. Speaking of playing, where is Kim? Ah, there you are. What's next on this list? I came to bet and take you rich people's money."

"How are you two even sisters?" McCaine asked. "She needs to come on the guys' trip to the casino next time."

Tammy pinched his leg. "Take a chill pill, old man."

Landon looked at Kim and mouthed, "Cut her off for the night."

Kim held up *OK* with her fingers.

Caleb twisted off the top of the beer with his bare hands and passed it to Launa. She patted the seat next to her and slid closer to Jay to make room for him.

"I think it's time we partner up and bring down the house. Whatdya say, Caleb?" Launa ran her fingers across his head.

He blushed. "Ey. I'm here with you."

"What are your friend's names again?" Todd asked Caleb.

"That right there is Coran. And that's Seth." Caleb adjusted his shirt from beneath his stocky arms.

"Seth, you look familiar to me. T, he look familiar to you?" Jay asked.

"Yeah, that's why I asked. But I can't put my finger on where."

"We'll figure it out before the night is over. I'm sure," Jay added.

Landon and Jen rolled their eyes at Jay and Todd's banter.

Kim put an end to Launa's display of being a bad guest and slid a drawing easel into the living room.

Derailed

"Time to test those art skills. Pictionary is up, but with a twist. We are going to draw names and pair up that way."

The guests sulked as Brian walked around the room with a hat filled with the male guest names on a folded piece of paper. The women pulled from the hat and revealed their new partner's name. The room was already full of jokes and laughter as they switched seats, and the odd pairs teamed up ready to play.

Landon partnered with Jay, Todd with Launa, Brian with Millicent, Seth with Tammy, Caleb with Shanice, Kim with Coran, and McCaine with Jen.

"We'll go first." Brian picked a card from the deck. He drew his best artwork of a man kneeling down on top of a fist, and an arm with muscles.

Millicent struggled to make sense of it and guessed incorrectly, "Neil Armstrong."

"No. It's Mike Tyson. It's a fist and muscles."

"But why is the man kneeling down instead of lying down?"

"Because I couldn't draw a man lying down."

"Next!" McCaine hit the wrong answer buzzer.

Todd went second and with ease drew a bird and a worm. Launa stood and calmly answered, "The Early Bird Gets The Worm." She and Todd high fived, then Launa belted out, "That's right, Bruh-law. Show 'em how it's done."

Shanice let out a loud sigh.

Coran took to the board and drew a circle, vigorously pressing the marker in the middle of it. The dot grew bigger each time he hit the easel. Kim shouted, "Center of the Universe!" Coran's eyes grew big when he nodded. Kim guessed, "On Point! Um, period in a circle! Point, blank, period!"

The timer dinged and Coran dropped his head. "It was center stage," he muttered.

"But where is the stage?" Kim asked.

"The circle is the stage. I was nodding yes when you said, "Center," but you moved on from that word.

"Well, good try." Kim frowned when his back turned.

Seth took to the board and showed off his art skills. Standing at six foot three, his skinny frame kneeled down to the board and drew a fast caricature of the rap artist Drake. Tammy guessed it correctly and everyone clapped at how great the drawing turned out.

Kim sprung from her chair and patted Seth on the back. "You are definitely invited back, and will be my partner next time. Can I keep this drawing?"

"If Landon doesn't want it. Sure." He blushed.

The room grew silent and all eyes shifted to Todd, looking at Landon's rosy cheeks with wounded eyes.

The offer and the silence tickled her. She said to Kim. "I'll let you have it since it's your party." Kim rolled up the drawing and tied a string around it with one of the ribbons from the gift bag. Landon turned to Seth. "But I would love to see your art collection and hang something on my wall."

"You got it." Seth winked at her.

"Who's next?" Todd huffed.

"That would be the best dressed motherfucker in the room." Jay stood up.

"Jay, I got this." Landon tapped his shoulder. "Just get it right."

She stepped to the podium and drew a devil, a pair of high heels, and a square with dollar signs inside.

Launa shouted, "Is it someone we know?"

Landon looked at Launa and begged for her to behave.

Jay silenced Launa and started yelling answers, "Money is the root of all evil! If it don't make money, it don't make sense! The devil don't fuck with broke bitches!"

Landon added the movie cut clapboard to her drawing, and a box of popcorn.

Jay jumped up and down and screamed, "*The Devil Wears Prada!*"

"Ah, hell nah. How would you know that?" Tammy fussed.

"I love me some Meryl Streep. That white lady can act."

The room went into chaos of laughter, and all the men stood and patted Jay on the back. Shanice stood, and the room fell silent. Too silent as everyone turned to Launa snickering in Todd's ear. She rolled her eyes at Launa as she drew a calendar, and a rain cloud. Caleb correctly guessed, "April Showers," and earned them a point.

McCaine jumped up from the floor and attempted to top Seth's drawing with his rendition of big hair, a television that looked like a robot, and a microphone that resembled an ice cream cone.

"I have no idea what a robot would be doing with an ice cream cone and wearing a wig, I'm guessing," said Jen.

"No. It's The Oprah Winfrey Show. Look at the hair. And this isn't a robot. It's a TV," McCaine explained.

"Okay one more round of this, then back to the card table," Brian told his guests.

The group played one more round of Pictionary with their dates and spouses, followed by a quick break to eat at the food table. Todd snuck looks at Seth making Landon laugh, waiting for her to lock eyes with him like they always did. He worked his way closer towards them, eavesdropping on their conversation.

"Is it possible I can see you again?" Seth asked Landon.

Todd interrupted. "Can I talk to you for a second? In private."

Seth answered, "The lady is still eating right now."

"I asked the lady. Not you." Todd flared his nostrils.

"I'm done eating. I'll be right back," Landon pinned her lips together towards Seth.

She followed Todd to the edge of the living room near the front door.

"Are you for real with this clown?" Todd pointed to Seth.

"It's not what it looks like."

"It looks like he is sizing you up. And he ain't good enough for you to be doing that."

"I'm only here with him because I heard you were bringing a date, and I didn't want to show up by myself. Shanice seems nice."

Todd stared in her eyes and exhaled a long breath. "You and I both know Launa has made sure I never see her again."

They both laughed.

"And she's not so nice. She's after money. And beginning to bore me."

"So why'd you bring her?"

"Same as you. Didn't want to show up by myself. You been good?"

"So so. And you? Well, don't answer that. I've heard how you've been doing. It's good seeing you. Friend."

"You too. Now don't make me beat that clown's ass tonight."

"Tell that to my sister." Landon pointed to Launa.

Launa saluted them with a drink and shimmied her way over towards Caleb. Todd and Landon cackled at her dance, then rejoined everyone back at the food table. Jay was overheard asking Jen about Jules.

"Where's Pretty Boy?"

"Turn on the television and see. You know the league plays on the holidays."

"That's right. I wasn't thinking about the games. I was really wondering where I've seen that Seth cat before, and what are you doing showing up with some random men?"

Derailed

"Why do you care who she's with?" Millicent asked.

"A man's gotta know who is being brought around his kid."

"Jay, I didn't take you as the kind to be questioned about your business," Launa butt in.

"Launa, this conversation has nothing to do with you." Millicent sucked her teeth.

"You're right. It was between him and her." Launa pointed to Jen and Jay. "So why are you in it? Snobby sneaky ass bitch."

"Whoa. Whoa. Did I miss something?" Jay asked.

"Now hold up. We won't have any of that tonight," said Brian.

"Yo, Landon's little sister, chill out." Jay slid her a drink.

"I'm cool." Launa smirked.

"I beg to differ. You've been taunting me all night." Shanice joined the debate.

"Shalice, is it?" said Launa.

"It's Shanice."

"Sorry, babes, you aren't even relevant." Launa laughed.

"That is my cue to leave before I beat a bitch's ass. Todd! Take me home."

"What is your problem, Launa?" Millicent frowned.

"Trust me. You don't want me to go there."

"Damn, is it time to call it a night already?" Tammy asked.

"But, baby, we haven't whipped their asses in Spades yet," McCaine complained. "I don't care if they knock each other out. I came to eat, drink, and play some cards. And afterwards go home and have butt naked sex on top of all of the money I won."

The tension died and everyone laughed. Launa apologized for her unkind words and made a promise. "From here on out, I'll be on my best behavior, and beat all of your asses in Spades. Let's do this!"

Todd walked over to Launa and whispered in her ear. "You made me laugh tonight, Little Sis. Look after my baby. And don't let that clown put a finger on her. I gotta take Shanice home. Love ya."

"Be safe out there on that road, Bruh-law. And Todd, do me a favor. Do better. Please?" Launa grinned.

Shanice yelled from the porch. "I can still hear her talking about me!"

"I better get going guys. I'll see y'all later." He tipped his head. "Landon."

Todd smirked at Seth on his way out and shared a smile with Landon as he opened the door for Shanice. He nudged her outside as she yelled, "She doesn't know me like that! And trust me she doesn't want to! I'll fuck up these nice people's house with her narrow ass!"

"Ooohhh she's mad now." Jay rubbed elbows with Launa. "Why did you pick at that girl like that?"

"I meant what I said. He could do better." Launa shuffled the deck. "Caleb dear, do you need me to get you anything before I deal?"

"I'm good, babe."

"Now that that's settled, I have something I want you to do for me."

"What's that?"

"Steal all of his books." Launa pointed to McCaine.

"Landon, come get your trouble making sister. She does not want none of this!" McCaine slapped the table.

"I'll follow your lead, mama." Caleb blew Launa a kiss.

Launa moaned. "Twenty bucks a game starts now."

As the card game commenced, Tammy tried to learn more about Seth and Coran. They gave Coran the third degree until Seth mentioned he was shy, and didn't talk much around people he didn't know.

"You weren't this quiet last night," said Jen.

"Y'all hung out last night?" Tammy asked.

Derailed

"Yeah, we had coffee downtown and took the girls ice skating. We had a good time," Seth replied.

"Wonder what Jules would say about that?" Jay chuckled.

"I haven't been ice skating in decades." Tammy spoke loud so McCaine could hear her at the table. "Why don't you take me ice skating anymore?"

"Because I need my hands to work and pay these bills! Now leave me alone. I'm concentrating."

Tammy fanned him off. "Excuses, excuses. Next time y'all go, invite us along."

"'Cause we sure weren't invited last night." Millicent sighed under her breath.

"I'm trying to get Landon here to tell me when she wants to go back out there and show me what she's got." Seth grinned in her face.

Jay cleared his throat and shouted, "I'll take that!"

The party gathered around the card table serving as the entertainment for the rest of the night. Landon was impressed at the card shark her sister had become. Launa's game matched her mouth, and Caleb had fallen in love with her fun girl persona, while Jay failed at hiding he was turned on by her hustling abilities.

The time passed one a.m. as the final hand of the night was dealt. "Take your sister back to the country," said McCaine, sweating from his armpits and shaking the table with his knees. Launa snatched another book from the table and smiled at McCaine, who was eyeing her like she was the devil.

"You don't know about them country girls." She laughed.

"I know bout'em." Caleb snarked.

Launa stared in Jay's eyes, and Millicent grew uneasy. With a poker face, she winked at Caleb to follow her lead, and played her final card. Caleb snatched the book and smacked the table. "Eight it up! Get up from the table!" Launa and Caleb eliminated McCaine and Jay— the first time in the history of their tag teaming efforts.

"That'll be $500," Launa said to Jay, winning a side bet from bypassing the points total.

Jay pulled out a wad of cash. "You have got one hell of a little sister, L. Y'all are like night and day."

"I'll teach you how to play one day, Jay." Launa held out her hand for her winnings.

"Well, this has been fun. Brian and I want to thank you all for coming. This one is in the books."

"Thank God this night is over. I don't know how much more I can take," Millicent mumbled.

"What are you griping about?" Landon asked her.

Millicent nodded at Launa. "Your sister has been on one. Taunting Todd's date. Coming in here with one guy, and flirting with Jay in my face. So disrespectful and unnecessary."

Jen laughed out loud.

"My sister was not flirting with Jay."

Launa put on her coat. "Lighten up, Millie. I'm here with someone. Whatchu so nervous about? Oh yeah. I forgot." Launa snickered.

"Like that! She's been saying slick shit like that all night!" Millicent argued.

Jay chimed in. "Launa, you are cool as fuck, but on the real you have been coming for folks pretty hard all night. My girl being one of them. What's up?"

"What's up is your girl is grimey and a fraud."

"Please enlighten me." Millicent clung to Jay.

"Landon, that issue we recently resolved back home, where I told you who my son's father was?"

"Yeah."

"Remember when I said I found out he was seeing multiple

girls, and the day I went to tell him I was pregnant I saw him kissing someone?"

"Yeah."

"It was your best friend." Launa pointed to Millicent. "She was fucking him too."

"So there's a pattern," Jen chimed in.

Landon's face turned bright red. "Why would you keep that from me after all of these years? Like you've had so many opportunities to tell me you did that."

Millicent sent daggers with her eyes across the room at Launa. "I didn't want it to come in between our friendship. You can't possibly hold that against me now. That was eons ago. Neither of us give a shit about that guy now. Landon, this is stupid."

"Fuck Reynaldo, this is about you being my friend. And Jen's friend. You did the same thing to both of us. I don't even know who you are anymore."

"Yes, you do. I'm your best friend. One mistake can't change that."

"I'm not so sure anymore. Kim and Brian, thanks for having us." Landon grabbed her coat and led everyone out.

Millicent stepped out into the cold calling Landon's name. Landon kept walking and hopped in the car with Jen in the driver's seat.

"Ain't no way in hell I'm letting Launa drive us home. How you feeling?"

"Confused. Like I can't trust anyone."

"Hmm. You can trust me, 'cause I damn sure trust you."

Launa and Caleb slammed into the side of the car, making out with condensation clouding around them.

Seth knocked on Landon's window. "I don't know what tonight was about, but if you ever wanna get together or talk, here's my number. Hope to hear from you."

"I'll give you a call," Landon lied and rolled up the window. "I have no intention of ever seeing him again."

Jen chuckled. "Your sister promised us tonight would be epic. She could have told us she was holding onto a hand grenade."

"Makes me wonder, what I would do if…Never mind. I'm not going down that road."

"So let me get this straight. The guy we talked about when you came to visit me turned out to be your sister's son's father, and fucked your best friend?"

"Yup."

"Ain't you glad you held your pussy hostage?"

Jen and Landon burst into a roaring laughter.

Launa hopped in the back seat. "Well, didn't I say we would have a good time tonight?" She waited for the two of them to pipe down. "Now you know she has the tendency to stab you in the back."

"You could have told me this months ago, ya know."

"Yeah, but I wanted to see her face when I exposed her secret. She has never liked me, and I have never liked her. She had too much influence on you growing up. You and I were thick as thieves, and then one day you and her became friends, and you pushed me to the side."

"That's not true. Well, maybe just a little."

"I forgive you." Launa squeezed her sister's shoulder.

"And I you."

"You two make me wish I had a sister." Jen's lips curved.

"You do. You have me." Landon pounded her fist.

"And me," Launa added. "You are the realest person Landon has hung out with. Welcome to the family!"

Chapter 25

Look At Us

Jen

Jules surprised Jen before her week ended in Detroit, proposing they fly to Vegas and elope. Jen's mind went blank for a second as flashes of Alex smiling at her from the grave formed tears in her eyes.

"I didn't mean to make you cry." Jules wiped her cheeks.

"I wasn't expecting you to ask so soon."

"Is that a yes?"

"Yes." Jen hesitated. "But Vegas?"

"At Christmas. That gives us a few weeks to get a plan sorted out. Whatdya say?"

"Something small and intimate."

"However you want it."

Before she shared the news, she questioned Max about his feelings for Jules and Millicent. His response would determine if she would go through with the wedding. To her surprise, Millicent was the victor of the two.

"I love Ms. Millicent. She reads to me a lot, and is nice to me, and tells me she loves me and my mommy every night."

Jen was shocked by Max's response. She reflected on the

memorable moments they shared, and figured with the care Millicent was providing for her son in her absence, she could forgive Millicent for being a backstabbing bitch, but would never forget it, and no longer harbored any hatred towards her. She thought, 'Was them falling in love a fluke?'

Still undecided on what to do, Jen kept the proposal from everyone. She returned to Miami with a racing mind, and spent days tallying the pros and cons of saying "I do," once again.

Jay called her to settle Max's schedule for the holidays. Jen had no choice but to come clean with her decision, and kept her word that she would explain to him why she said what she said the day they put their differences aside.

"Can you come down here, so we can talk?"

"In person? Is that necessary?"

"It is. You should come see where we live."

"I'll call you when I get in town."

The urgency in Jen's voice was recognizable from the years they spent together. Millicent wasn't pleased he was leaving on short notice, or where he was headed, and acted out.

"Are you done playing with me, and now chasing what you've lost?" she asked.

"Stop your worrying. I'll be back soon. And I'm coming home to you."

"Is Jen in some sort of trouble? Can I help?"

"Why would you think that?"

"Just be careful. And tell her I miss her and I still love her. Even if she hates me."

Knowing Jen's secret, Millicent did have something to worry about. If Jen was getting Jay involved with her hellish past, she feared the worst for everyone involved, and Jay could see in her eyes she knew something he didn't. He touched down in Miami and followed Jen's directions, meeting at a hotel on South Beach.

They walked a long way from the hotel to a secluded location past the strip, where the waves could distort the sound. Jen looked over her shoulder repeatedly making Jay nervous.

"Why did I have to leave my phone at the hotel? Should I have brought my gat or something?"

"Sorry. What I have to say can't be said near a phone, and I'm always on alert. I'm surprised you never noticed."

"What's going on, Jen? You got a brother on edge coming down here by himself."

"I wanted to run a few things by you."

"I do as well." Jay looked over his shoulder.

"Jules asked me to marry him, and I said yes."

"You're gonna marry the pretty boy? I didn't think it would last this long. When?"

"Christmas in Vegas. Max will be out of school for the holidays, so it all works out."

"Are you sure this is the guy for you?"

"It feels right." She smiled. "I feel loved."

"I'm coming at you with nothing but truth, girl. I don't like him. I've tried, but I follow my gut, and I just can't put my finger on it. You call me shady all the time. Well maybe shady knows shady like real knows real. I feel like he is a pretender. And I don't want to see you get hurt. If dude hurts you, I'm going to hurt him. That's my word."

"Unfortunately, I'm the pretender."

Jay stopped walking and looked in Jen's eyes. She confessed her true identity and told him what she'd endured before he came into her life. As he listened, he saw a version of himself staring back at him. In that moment he realized why they were compatible more as friends than lovers, as they both kept secrets, and both couldn't be trusted in their relationship.

As Jen wrapped up her story involving the money, the murder, and her menacing mother, she revealed she knew he and Todd's hands were dirty.

Jay laughed. "You don't know nothin' girl."

"I know more than you think. That's why I'm having this conversation with you. I followed you a few times before I caught you cheating. I know about the gambling ring where y'all fight cocks, the number houses, the sporting bets, and the you-know-what."

Jay rubbed his goatee. "Is that right?"

Jen lifted her blouse. "I'm not wearing a wire. I don't need you to deny or confirm. I'm bonding with you. I may need you to come through for me one day."

"Why do you say?"

"I'm going to go after the money." Her face turned grave.

"Are you nuts? You don't know anything about that country. The laws are different. The streets are foreign. We know nothing about that place, or how they operate."

"I didn't say I was going now, but one day I will, and I might call on you. Will you answer?"

"I'm not going over there." Jay spoke with his chest.

"What are you afraid of?"

"Why aren't you afraid is a better question?"

Jen turned around and led the way back to the hotel. Jay repeated his question.

Jen huffed. "Because it's mine. And my daddy lost his life behind it."

"Doesn't mean you need to lose yours. You have more than enough, I'll see to it you never go without. Leave that shit where it is." Jay grabbed her hand. "Look, a part of me will always love you, but I'm thinking we didn't work out because I didn't know the real you, and I thought you didn't know the real me. And maybe that's what broke us. But you and Max are always gonna be my responsibility. I'm here for you if you need me. But leave that shit over there with them people."

"I'll give it some more thought."

"In the meantime, send a pic of your boy to my phone just in case he ain't who you think he is."

"I will when we get back to the hotel. Now what did you want to run by me?"

"Where do you stand these days on Millicent?"

"We're all human and allowed to make mistakes I suppose."

"Did somebody body snatch the Jen I know? Who are you and what have you done with my son's mother?" Jay joked. "But on the real, she loves you and Landon. Talks about y'all all the time. I'll be glad when you three make up, and shit can go back to the way it used to be."

"One day. Maybe?"

"Women have the hardest time letting shit go. Look at me down here on pretty boy island. Be like me. Let it go."

Jen laughed. "I don't hate her. You might get your wish soon enough. So how do you like it down here?"

"It's alright. But I'm catching the red eye back out tonight."

"Why?"

"This is ain't my stomping grounds, and these ain't my streets."

Jen nodded her head. "Some things about you will never change, but I noticed a few things are different about you."

"Like what?"

"You seem happier. A little more free and settled."

"It took for you to leave me to look at myself."

"And maybe Millicent had something to do with it. She's good for you. You and Max."

Jay narrowed his eyes on Jen. "Again, where is the Jen I know?"

"I'm happy now."

"Seems so. Are you gonna tell your soon to be husband about the business venture before or after y'all are married?"

"After."

Jay shook his head. "Have it your way. It will be a few months, but once all the leg work is complete, I'll fly you out to see it. Then you can take it from there."

"Can't wait."

"Look at us, working as a team." Jay grinned.

"Max would be proud."

Chapter 26

Peace of Mind

Jay

Hours before the red eye delivered Jay back to Michigan, he made the most of his short trip with a business dinner in the city and caught the game at the arena where Jules worked. His associates treated him to the hottest strip club in the Miami nightlife. And after being entertained by drinks and slutty women, he flew home with a lot to think about from a night to remember.

The sky was still dark when Millicent welcomed him in their bed. Wide awake, wearing nothing but a smile, she pulled the covers back. "I prayed you'd make it back in one piece. How did it go?"

"It went well. I have some things to process, and work on with Todd, but overall things are looking up," he replied.

"Did she tell you anything new?"

"Let's just say we got everything out in the open."

"Did y'all talk about us?"

"We did."

"And?"

"Like I said, things are on the up and up."

"What does that mean?"

"Give it time, Mills. It will work itself out."

"If you say so. What is that smell on you?"

"The beach, booze, and bitches from the strip club."

"Strip club? You can't be serious coming in here with heaux juice all over you. Get out of my bed."

"Your bed?"

"It became my bed when I moved in here and had it delivered. So yes, my bed."

"Come here, girl. I like that feistiness." Jay slid her to the bottom of the bed by her feet.

"Don't touch me with those nasty ass hands either." Millicent pushed him away. "Is this where it begins to end for me?"

"What are you talking about?"

"Am I going to have to count condoms and worry you are out there cheating on me with ratchet bitches and heauxs in the club too?"

"Slow down with that. I caught a game, dinner, drinks and went to the club with some business associates. I have never cheated on you. I got what I want, and I'm wiser now. You gotta leave my past in the past if you want to be my future. You hear me?"

"I hear you, but I am not listening."

"This dick belongs to Millicent St. James. You listening to that?"

Millicent kicked back to the top of the bed.

"I'm going to take a shower, and when I get back I'm going to write my name all over your ass. You'll hear me, feel me, and listen to me then."

He rushed back to Millicent dripping wet with his gear in shift. They tumbled and tussled for a few rounds, while Jay pled his case for trustworthiness. "You think your man has been

Derailed

tipping out? You need your man to prove his love for you?" Millicent resisted his kisses and didn't answer. Jay groped and tickled and fondled her until she folded with low screeches.

"Okay, okay I believe you."

"Good. I don't want you to ever think I'm being disloyal to you, Mills. You are the woman for me."

Jay placed his vodka infused lips on hers and kissed her sloppy, rough, and long. The thought of her walls had been on his mind during his flight home, and he played out what he imagined now that she was in his grasp.

Clutching her ass tightly from below, he *grinded* on top of her, fighting his penis to stop the quick entry it aimed for. It bounced and shifted side to side, ready to feel her slick lips gyrate around him. The plans to taste her walls were forced to wait as his mind lost the battle to his dick. It forged inside of her pussy, pushing and pulling as she quietly "Aaahed" in his ear.

Rough from the start, she held onto his shoulders, her nails scraping his back while her body welcomed the lashing. Jay was lost in a euphoric state listening to her pant and gasp for air, digging deeper and deeper in her world. He grinned at the extra warmth drizzling on his pipe. The vodka in his system added to his stamina, giving him the power to fuck her long and hard, fast then slow, slipping and sliding inside her walls, weakening her with broad strokes until she quietly released sounds of ecstasy into the pillows.

The sun was now high above the trees, but the pound fest was far from over. Millicent laid wrecked on top of the bed she bragged about. Jay removed the pillow from her face and placed his hands over her mouth, continuing a high performance of rigorous strokes to the back of her wall, while fingering her clit. Millicent moaned and bit his hand, shivering below him like a razor in a barber's hand. Jay fucked his liquored soul to his peak. He grabbed her withered body and grunted, pressing his face against hers. "I love you," he whispered in her ear.

"I want more of that when I wake up," she said.

Jay laughed, looking at the clock. "Then that's in ten minutes."

Chapter 27

Moving Forward
Jen

As requested, Landon escorted Max to Las Vegas for Jen and Jules' big day with Launa and Laura Lee as a surprise.

"I couldn't let you go on lockdown forever without showing you the best night of your life," said Launa.

"Maybe." Landon frowned. "It's Christmas, and we can't let her walk down the aisle looking tired and beat."

"And we still need to check the venue. How about a post-marital night on the town next time we're together?"

Jen hugged the girls. "I like the sound of that."

The trio visited the hotel's wedding chapel in the heart of the building. An intimate, beautifully decorated gazebo filled with colorful bouquets of lilies surrounded by candles couldn't have been more pleasing. "So much better than the first time," Jen mumbled.

Ms. Rosetti, Jules's mother, arrived to survey the chapel. She looked at Jen as if it were the first time they'd met. "We should have met you a long time ago. Who can get to know a person the day before a wedding?" she grumbled. Jen got the sense she pretended not to know her because she disapproved of her family's history. She gave Launa and Landon a look of concern and laughed nervously. Launa stepped in as the family Jen needed to support her against her future mother-in-law, throwing subtle jabs back at her so Jen didn't have to.

"A wedding in Vegas. The place of sin," Ms. Rosetti complained.

"The place of love. Where your son chose to get married. Not Jen," Launa answered.

"When do we meet the boy?"

"'The boy' has a name, Max. And you'll meet him tomorrow, at your son's wedding, and it will be beautiful." Launa cringed with a smile.

The tone of Jules's mother heightened. "And who are you?"

"I'm Launa, Jen's baby sister. Nice meeting you."

After the hostile meet and greet, the Davis sisters met in Jen's bridal suite. They decorated a miniature Christmas tree and exchanged gifts early. Jen clung on to Max, taking in every moment with him to make up for the time she missed.

"Max is going to have three Christmases this year. Tonight, when we get back to my house, and at his dad's house." Landon tousled his hair. "Did I tell you an elf dropped off some presents for you at my house this morning before we left?"

Max's eyes grew big.

"Speaking of gifts..." Launa went to the closet. "An elf dropped this off for you."

Launa handed Landon a gift bag from one of the boutiques downstairs in the hotel. She frustrated everyone, carefully untying the red ribbon, feeling for the tape on the edge so she didn't tear the paper.

"We'll be here all day." Laura Lee sighed.

Landon opened the card taped to the box and read it aloud:

Derailed

"Making sure you have something under your tree.
Merry Christmas
~Love Todd"

She opened the box and held the latest Louboutin bag to her chest. A tear formed in her eyes, and Laura Lee passed her a tissue from her purse.

"I can't keep this."

"How long are you going to make that man suffer?" her mother asked.

"That's not my intention, Mama. I thought we were finally making progress as friends."

"He doesn't want to be your friend, chile. He wants to be your husband."

Landon felt guilty. She had broken her vows and broken his heart, but reached a comfortable place with having him in her life without having to deal with his baggage.

"When did Todd put you up to this?"

"A few days ago when he found out you weren't going to be home for Christmas. What are you going to do?" Launa asked.

"Definitely send him a Christmas gift, but I think I might have to cut off all communication for a while, or I'll never move on."

"And neither will he." Launa squeezed her sister's shoulder.

* * *

Like sisters would do, Landon and Launa showed up at Jen's door in the morning with coffee in hand, ready to tend to their maid duties. They ordered a light breakfast for the bride, prepped for her dressing with hair and makeup, and made sure Max looked sharp to carry the rings.

Time stood still in the room when an unexpected knock

sounded at the door. "We're coming down in five minutes!" Launa yelled. The knock startled them again. She counted everyone in the room. "We're all here. Who the hell is being an asshole at the door?"

She opened it and gasped. "Of course." Launa chuckled. "What are you doing here, Millicent?"

"I come bearing gifts and apologies. If you all will have me."

"Come in," said Jen, surprising Landon and Launa.

Millicent hugged her and passed out cards and gifts.

"I'm glad you came. I've been meaning to call you, but things moved so fast I never got the time. I forgive you, and would like it very much if you would come to my wedding."

Max entered the room and hugged Millicent. When Jen saw the happiness on her son's face, she knew she had done the right thing, and took it as a sign of good faith that the day was going to be beautiful.

"How about you?" Millicent asked Landon.

Jen tapped Millicent on the shoulder. "It takes time, Millicent. Quit while you're ahead."

Landon withdrew and smiled to herself in the corner. It felt good to know Jen had her back and silenced Millicent so she didn't have to. Launa exhaled and took control of the room. "Ready?" she asked Jen. She nodded, and followed her team downstairs to her ceremony.

Jules lifted his bride in the air after the minister declared, "I now pronounce you man and wife." He kissed her as their witnesses celebrated them, stopping the lip lock when Max pulled at the back of his tuxedo.

The guests laughed at Max's protection of his mom. Jules took his hand and placed it inside his mother's, covered theirs with his, and kissed them both. It was the first time Max looked him in the eye and smiled, bringing the room to tears.

In a separate suite, the happy couple held a small reception

Derailed

for their guests. The Rosettis disappeared to Jen's bridal suite for a quickie in her wedding gown. The tulle on her dress was flipped above her waist for twenty hard pumps and back at her feet before the guests could worry about their whereabouts. When they returned to their party, they danced in the middle of the room.

"That is the only time I'll forgive you for that driveby." Jen kissed her husband's ear.

"That is the only time I plan to rush tearing that wet ass up."

They laughed forehead to forehead.

"I wonder if this is how most couples talk to each at their wedding?" Jen whispered.

"I don't know. But I bet most husbands are thinking what I'm thinking."

"Which is?"

"I wish these people weren't around so I can fuck the shit out of my wife again."

The couple laughed hysterically in the middle of the dance floor. As the chuckles settled, Jen noticed Launa tossing her braids in front of Jules's brother, Juan, while Millicent babysat Max, and Landon kept Laura Lee company. She took one final look around the room and laid her head on her husband's chest.

"Today couldn't have been more perfect."

"It's not over yet. You ready to get out of here?"

"I am."

Their party threw rice and rose petals when they exited the front entrance of the hotel. Jen tossed her bouquet directly to Landon, blew her a kiss, and cried as she waved goodbye with her new husband on her arm. Landon caught the kiss in the air and smelled the lilies in the bouquet. She looked up at Jen. "Thank you," she said under her breath, hoping the happiness she saw in her friend would extend her way.

Chapter 28

Press Your Luck

Millicent

Launa decided to come up for air from Jules's brother and try her hand in the casino before they left Vegas. She ran into Millicent trying out her luck on the slots.

"I thought you left town?" Launa plopped down in the seat next to her nemesis.

"Nope. Enjoying some me time."

"Trouble in paradise?"

"You would love that, wouldn't you?" Millicent rolled her eyes. "Unfortunately for you, everything is just fine at home. I saw you had that cute guy all over you earlier."

"Yeah I did. Didn't I?" Launa polished her nails with her shirt.

"Jules's brother, right?"

"Yup."

"What happened with you and that guy you brought to game night?"

"He's still around. I don't have a ring on this finger." Launa flipped her hand front to back.

"Very smart. Until there is a ring on it, you can't put a claim on it."

A waitress approached carrying a tray of complimentary champagne. Each took a flute from the tray and sipped.

"Tangy," Launa exhaled.

"Cheap," said Millicent. "I believe this is the first real conversation you and I have ever had, Launa."

"I think you're right. It was because I didn't like you."

"And what, you like me now?" Millicent sneered at Launa.

"I didn't say that, but you coming out here to show Jen some love and apologize to my sister makes me see you a little different."

"I miss them both. They were like sisters to me."

"I know how that feels. You took my sister from me, but I'm over it now since we put all of that behind us."

"Launa, whatever I did to make you hate me so much, I apologize for it. Truce?"

"Thank you. That's all you had to say. And stop there before you kill my buzz."

"So are we good?"

"We're good."

"Will you help me get back in good with your sister?"

"I'm not getting in the middle of that. Let her hold her grudge for a while. Time will have to heal that wound," Launa advised. "I'm curious, though. Why didn't you tell her about you and Reynaldo?"

Millicent lowered her head and took a deep breath. "Have you ever regretted doing something stupid?"

"Ugh, hello. I love my kid, but if I could pick another daddy for him I would jump inside a time machine."

"Well, I was mad at myself after it happened. I felt like the biggest dummy alive. He saw me at the store, and we got to talking, and all I could think about was how Landon described what it looked like. I wanted to see if it really was as pretty as she said it was, so when he put the moves on me I went to his house. He whipped it out, and I was mesmerized. Next thing I knew, I was added to the hit list, and never heard from him again."

"It truly is a work of art attached to the most vile human being," Launa added. "And he talks a good game, doesn't he?"

Millicent shivered. "If you find that time machine, swing by and pick my ass up."

"Will do."

They clinked glasses.

"Alright, enough of that. Let's make a toast," Launa suggested. "Here's to good sex."

Millicent laughed and raised her glass. "To good sex I wish I could give back."

"And may I get some tonight."

"Launa, you are crazy as hell."

"People tell me that all the time. See you 'round."

Chapter 29

Curves

LAndon

Landon handled her first New Year's Eve as a divorced, single woman with a bottle of melatonin gummies, silk pajamas, and a bedtime before the clock struck midnight. The winter storm blowing in from the west was too brutal for anyone to get in or out of the city, and everyone was buried behind white ice castles and mounds of frozen snow.

A neighbor's kid made a few bucks off of Landon shoveling her snow and tending to her yard, clearing a path for her to get in and get out. Landon paid him handsomely as the months went on, but also treated him to the baked cakes, cookies, and pies she began baking on the regular to soothe her loneliness.

She became a fan of comfort food, and a Food Network enthusiast. If it looked good, she cooked it, and baked it, and fried it, and ate it. And if she couldn't make it, she ordered it to be delivered to her doorstep.

Her workout room turned into a dust haven, and her waistline nonexistent. It wasn't until winter was over that she noticed she was on the pudgy side. She'd put on so much weight, her clothes size went up by four, and her ass was so plump, men stopped whatever they were doing to stare. Todd couldn't believe his eyes when he ran into her.

"And I thought you couldn't get any prettier," he said, admiring her curves.

"You're being kind. How are you?"

"I would ask the same, but I see you're doing fine. I heard you put on some weight, but damn Landon, I like the extra roundness on that ass. You got some baby making hips on you now."

Landon twisted and moved her hands nervously. "Life treating you good?"

"It is today." Todd licked his lips.

Landon chuckled. "Well it was nice running into you. I might see you at the next party."

"You sure about that? You haven't come around since Thanksgiving."

"I just needed to take some time for myself. I'll be back around in time."

"I hope so. I heard you and Mills aren't on speaking terms. Do yourself a favor, and stop pushing away everyone who loves you." Todd winked.

"I'll keep that in mind."

Landon knew she went up a few sizes in her clothes, but it wasn't until Todd pointed out how much weight she gained that she decided to throw away her sweet tooth, and find the woman she used to be.

The calendar said spring, but the weather said not yet. Snow continued to fall, so Landon got a head start on her weight loss by dusting off her equipment in Todd's old man cave. When the treadmill became boring, she danced in a Zumba class, working off the pounds twice a week, and once on the weekend.

* * *

Derailed

Spring arrived past its due date. Landon jumped to the opportunity of neighborhood runs once the snow melted, and participated in weekend charity races. By summer she had run the twenty pounds she gained off of her, and had come to love the way running made her feel physically and mentally.

She continued to run regularly to maintain her figure, or whenever she felt anxious to turn on the oven and whip up something sweet.

Expanding her range of charities to donate to and stay in shape, she signed up for a race near the Eastern Market where the neighborhood had been gentrified, and the vendors sold fresh produce. The competition was fierce in that district, pushing her far from the front of the pack, but motivated her to return to compete with the best.

She placed closer to the front on her second race at the market, meeting some new friends to broaden her horizons. She tagged along with them to the market afterwards, flipping through the hues of green and yellow vegetables, and ripe fruit. Sweaty from the race, she hurried to make a decision on what to buy for the week before someone got a whiff of her workout.

Landon didn't know what possessed her to follow those people to the market without showering first. She hid below her hat, thumbing through the carrots, and stepped on someone's foot. "Sorry," she said without looking up, and nudged past the person.

"No need to apologize," a man's voice replied.

She reached for a batch of broccoli, and brushed against the fingers of another shopper. She lifted the brim of her hat, and the voice from before spoke.

"Oh, hey you."

"Hi." Landon smiled, showing all of her teeth.

"Landon, right?"

"You remembered my name."

"Of course I remembered your name. A man never forgets the name of a pretty woman. Especially one who was kind enough to bring him out of the rain. How are you?"

Landon blushed below her hat. "I'm doing good. What brings you this way?"

"My unit sponsored a race here this morning."

"Small world. I ran that race. You didn't mention you run before."

"Since I was in the marines, I run every day if I can. I don't know how I missed you out there." Walt sneakily checked out her physique. "Pardon me for asking, but do you always run without your wedding band?"

Landon fidgeted with her ring finger. "I'm actually divorced now."

"Sorry to hear that."

"It's okay. We are still good friends. Just no longer a ball and chain."

"I hate to hear you and your husband split up, but I can't say that doesn't make me smile. I'm sorry if that's weird." He gazed at her eyes peeking at him below her brim.

"Not weird at all." Landon's top teeth sank into her bottom lip.

"I know I don't live around here, but is it okay if I call you sometime. Maybe take you out to dinner?"

"I would love that."

"Here is my card. If you'll accept it this time." Walt laughed.

Landon read it and placed it in her pocket.

"I hope to hear from you." He slowly strolled away.

"You will."

Landon beamed from ear to ear. Running brought her back to life and helped her find herself again. It reintroduced her to the feeling of self-worth, and snapped her out of her obsession with food that masked her depression. It freed her mind and her waistline, and now it had introduced her to someone she could share all of that with— Detective Walter Reed, the man she rooted for her estranged best friend to give a chance. But as it turned out, the odds were in her favor, and when he came knocking this time, he'd be knocking for her, and her boots if he played his cards right.

Sneak Peek

Continue to enjoy a sneak peek of the final book in the On Track but Off Course Series

THE CROSSING

TEA

Landon

Turning heads as always, Landon arrived for a mandatory lunch date with Tammy, who wouldn't take no for an answer.

"We haven't seen you, *Ms.* Jeffries." Tammy stood, kissing the air next to her cheeks. "Looking good as always. You're glowing so bright I can see a halo above your head."

"I missed you, too." Landon hugged her.

"I tried to get you on the phone yesterday. I'm surprised you showed up today. Everyone thinks you've written us off."

Landon stuttered, "I—I have a good excuse. Tell everyone I've been super busy."

"When you stutter like that you are telling a quick one. I see being a horrible liar hasn't changed. What's really going on?"

Landon peered at Tammy with a side eye.

Tammy danced in her chair and slid her hands together. "Ooh. This ought to be good."

"It's not *what's* been keeping me busy. More like *who*?"

"Well, I know it isn't your former maintenance man, who still talks about you every-damn-time I walk in on the guys having a moment. His face lights up at the mention of your name."

A blended grin and resting bitch face curved on Landon's lips. "That was a mouthful."

"Yes, it was." Tammy sipped from the glass of water in front of her.

"And no, it's not him. I couldn't continue to see Todd and function properly. I had to cut off all ties with him in order to move on. Believe it or not, he made it easy for me to cut him loose the last time I saw him."

"How?"

"Can you believe he said he heard I had put on weight, and was loving how the thickness looked on me? Who the hell says that to a woman?"

"But he said you looked good?"

"What if the extra pounds *didn't* look good on me?"

"Ah. I see your point. Now enough of this deflection. Who is the mystery man you're keeping a secret? I promise I will keep it in the vault."

"Please, and do not use this as pillow talk tonight."

Tammy coiled her pinky around Landon's. "I give you my word."

"The man I'm seeing is kind, attentive, generous, sexy, athletic, good-looking, well-mannered."

"I'm waiting for you to stutter because all of that sounds like a lie. If it's too good to be true, it probably is." Tammy gasped. "It better not be a married man, Landon."

"He's not married, and you've met him already."

"The slim guy who could draw that you brought to the party last year?" Tammy guessed.

"No, not him."

Tammy sat back and huffed, struggling with the mystery. The long pause and smile on Landon's face tickled her, so she gave up as her mind went blank.

"I'm stumped. I don't recall seeing you with anyone besides the artist, and I'm bored with this guessing game."

Landon stained the glass of water sitting in front of her with the red paint on her lips and whispered, "His name is Walter."

Tammy frowned. "When did I meet anyone named Walter?"

Landon raised her eyebrows and took another sip.

"Wait a minute." Tammy leaned forward. "The cop Millicent ghosted was named...Get the hell out of here!"

"See my dilemma?"

"How in the hell did that happen?"

"We ran into each other at a charity race—Literally bumped into one another. He remembered my name, asked why I wasn't wearing my wedding band, and if he could take me out. I've been under him for weeks now." Landon stared at the floor in a daze, smiling to herself while drawing circles in the middle of her chest.

Tammy watched her get lost in her thoughts, chuckling at the goofy grin on her face that resulted in her cheeks turning rosy. A moment of silence crept between them with Tammy observing the early signs of love blooming. She remembered that look. The feeling of butterflies fluttering in the stomach, and recognized the entranced look in Landon's eyes.

"Do I dare ask where you went just now?" Tammy snapped her fingers.

Landon's grin blossomed into a smile.

"You're falling." Tammy lowered her voice. "Refresh my memory. Millicent never hooked up with him, right?"

"Nope. She hooked up with Jay instead."

"How long do you think you can keep this a secret?"

"Why does anyone have to know?"

"Because we're your friends, and you know you can't bring him around us."

"Eh." Landon shrugged her shoulders.

"It's only been a few weeks, but surely you remember Jay. He will clown that poor man. You know how he is."

"I couldn't care less to be honest."

"This guy must really be something."

"He is. I wasn't expecting to meet anyone like him, when you know, I already had one great love. How the hell did I get two?"

"Love?"

"I'm speaking too soon, I know. But when I say I've been under him since the day we met—I'm being literal. He called me an hour after we ran into each other, and brought me some chocolate covered strawberries a few hours later. I left him standing at the front door while I put them in the fridge. When I came back so we could leave, he softly kissed me on my lips and said, 'I didn't want to wait until the end of the night to do that. I couldn't help myself.'"

"Well okay then."

"Right!" Landon tapped Tammy's hand. "Then, he opened my car door, and kissed me again before taking my hand and seating me. I was wet before we pulled out of my driveway. He had me flustered sitting across from him at dinner thinking about those kisses."

"Damn, Landon. It's getting hot at this table." Tammy fanned herself. "Please go on."

"At dinner I learned he doesn't have any children, major points for me, and he has never been married."

"Did you discuss Millicent at all?"

"Not once. Anyway, while we were waiting on the valet to bring his car around he said, 'I wish the night didn't have to end so soon.' Then I said, 'It would be a shame for you to drive back home tonight. You could stay at my place.'"

"And he did," Tammy muttered.

Landon chuckled. "Then he said, 'It would be impossible for me to stay at your place in another room and get any rest knowing you are close by.' Then I said, 'Who says you have to stay in another room?'"

Tammy covered her mouth. "This is so unlike you."

"It is, isn't it? I don't know what got into me, but I'm glad he did. We stopped by the store to get some eggs, juice, snacks like cupcakes and chips, and protection." Landon muttered the latter.

"Good girl."

"You should have seen how the lady at the checkout was grinning at me, and looking at him and the condoms. After he paid her, she winked at me and whispered, 'Go get'em, girl.' And boy did I ever. We made it back to my house, and he followed me into the kitchen. He put the groceries away and snuck behind me in the pantry. His lips hovered over mine as he gazed into my eyes, breathing in all of my air. We kissed—hard this time, and he didn't let go of my lips so easily like before. He drew my tongue from my mouth and held it hostage, picked me up, and came up for air to ask me which way to the bedroom. I pointed upstairs, and everything after was fucking magical."

"Are you sure? Because you haven't had sex in months. Close to a year if I remember correctly. Could it have been that your body was appreciative of being touched by strong hands?"

"Tammy, the man laid me across my new bed and stared into my eyes, slowly pacing himself as he undressed me. The anticipation of what was to come was sexy. It was like I was being seduced while he read my mind, planning what he was going to do to me. The man was in tune with my mind and my body."

Tammy smirked at Landon.

"Why are you looking at me like that?"

"I'm waiting for you to stutter."

"You'll be waiting forever." Landon exhaled. "This man traced my lips with his finger, and told me to relax while he ran downstairs. He came back with one of the cupcakes and spread the icing across my breasts. His lips felt like magic going across my nipples like a slow midnight train taking its time with my body, careful when speeding across all major bumps with intricate soft kisses and finger play–locking his eyes with mine to study my reaction."

Tammy interrupted. "I'm going to need a drink listening to this." She hailed the waiter. "One peach margarita, please."

The waiter scurried off and Tammy begged for Landon to continue.

"After the slow burn of teasing, and fingering, and tracing my body from head to toe, he rolled the condom on. I'm thinking he's about to put it in, but he lifted my ass up in the air, grated my cheeks with his teeth, and tongued me everywhere. Blew my fucking mind! I was done. But he wasn't. Out of nowhere he slipped inside of me and touched every corner that needed dusting." Landon clutched her hands around her glass of water, stroking the sweat lubing the outside.

"I'm speechless," said Tammy.

"So was I. After he came the first time I was thinking we are going to roll over and go to sleep. I was wrong. He went downstairs and brought up the strawberries, and fed them to me. Had me licking chocolate off of his fingers which led to a second round. I straddled on to him and rode him like my life depended on it, and when I was done, he got back on top and finished himself off without my help. I was too weak to assist. Now here's the freaky part." Landon's cheeks rosed. "He went back down on me after we both came, and tongued my pussy like it was my mouth until I came again. But what has me so fucked up is after I was shaking like an earthquake, he rubbed my body with deep thrusts of his wrist. I have never been so relaxed in my life. He then took me by the chin and turned my face towards him. He stared into my eyes as he gently swept his hands across my face, caressing me in one arm while the hand on the other massaged my scalp until I passed out. Have you ever had that done?"

TEA

"I can't say that I have. Is it possible to put it in a bottle so women can open it as needed?"

Landon laughed. "The next thing I knew it was morning and he was cooking me an omelet."

"Well I'll be damned. A unicorn that fucks your brains out and cooks? I might need to trade Caine's ass in. Does he have a brother?"

"Nope. One sister."

"After hearing all of this, I assume you were being catered to yesterday, which is why you ignored my call?"

"Sort of. We were active yesterday, but he was also helping me fix a few cracks he found around the house."

"Is that why you mentioned the love word?"

Landon sighed as she smiled. "This isn't a fling or a one night stand as you can see. The man woke me this morning with a foot rub. He said he loves me. I believe him."

"But do you love him?"

Own The Series

Floral Discreet Cover Options

REVIEWS ENCOURAGE VORACIOUS INTEREST EVERY WHERE TO SUPPORT
ME, THE AUTHOR

I GREATLY APPRECIATE IT

About the Author

T.K. RICHARDS is a multi-genre author of women's fiction and romance, featuring popular novels and novellas in Black Romance, Interracial/Multicultural Romance, Paranormal Romance, and YA Fiction. You can find her serialized fiction work on the Kindle Vella app. A graduate of Limestone University, T.K. has honors in Expository Writing, and was also the Poet Laureate of her graduating class. When she is not writing, she is immersed in the world of tennis, and binge watching movies—mostly comedy as she loves to laugh.

You can follow T.K. RICHARDS on the platforms listed below to interact with her personally:

- facebook.com/Tkrichards
- twitter.com/tkrichards1
- instagram.com/t.k.richards
- tiktok.com/@tkrwrites
- youtube.com/tkrichards
- goodreads.com/T.k.richards
- bookbub.com/authors/t-k-richards
- amazon.com/author/Tkrichards

Thank you for following the story of this ensemble cast in The On Track But Off Course Series. Prepare for the crossover of this series with my Hummus series this Christmas, 'Levi & Launa Find Love'.

For more information about T.K. Richards, personalized orders, access to special deals, audio, character merchandise, and events, visit www.tkrichards.com and subscribe to my newsletter: https://tkrichardsnewsletter.ck.page

Join My ARC Team

Join my ARC team here:
https://tkrarcteam.ck.page/

Top Selling Romance Books by T.K. Richards

An Affair Abroad

The Vampiress

Juke: A Love Story

Made in the USA
Columbia, SC
01 March 2024